GUARDED BY LOVE

SHANICEXLOLA

Before you proceed, please note that some parts of this book are arousing, adventurous, and downright raunchy. I encourage you to read with an open mind to thoroughly enjoy the passion within.

xoxo, ShanicexLola

Synopsis

The odds were stacked against us, but I was destined for him.

The way he catered to every part of me heightened my outlook on love. I wouldn't dare deny that his allurement was a gift from a prevailing force up above... until she showed up at our front door, willing to fight for him.

D é j à V u

You felt familiar the moment I met you.
A lovely sort of déjà vu.
When we spoke or laughed or danced, I became
overwhelmed by the powerful sensation that I had
been here before. And when we kissed, I felt the
energies of a thousand lives on our lips, like our
souls had known each other all along.

Beau Taplin | | D é j à V u

Donovan traced his fingertips along the neon, green choker around my neck. A compliment to my chocolate skin came in the form of a soft kiss on my cheek.

"What can I cook you for breakfast?" he asked. "You can have whatever you'd like." Intertwining his fingers between mine, he reeled my body closer to his.

Six beautiful months into our relationship had changed my life. The way Donovan catered to every part of me heightened my outlook on love.

Love

I'd always wholeheartedly believed in it. Quite honestly, I'd put myself last to it many times. The share of heartbreak I'd endured was unfair!

But *this*!

This was worth it. Meeting and falling in love with a man of Donovan's caliber was life-changing. He highlighted the good surrounding me. With him around, things hit different, like a persistent burst of sunshine.

"Is that right?" I enclosed my arms around his neck. His beard tickled my cheek. Pulling back to look up at his handsome face, I blushed at his thoughtful guise.

Donovan straightened his posture and towered over me. "You know it is." He nodded. "What's on your mind, beautiful?"

"Just wondering how I got so lucky." Lifting his hand to my lips, I rubbed my full lips over the top of it before holding it to my face. "He's charming. Attentive. Thoughtful. And he cooks? How'd I land one of Louisville's most popular chefs?"

"Chill with all that. You don't ever need to hype me. Having you by my side is hype enough. You make me look good."

"Tell me about it," I lifted on my toes to whisper against his lips. Whisking me off my feet, he sat me on the countertop next to the stove, then raided the refrigerator for fresh items to make one of his infamous omelets. "Donovan, you don't have to cook.

I'll pick up something quick on my way to the office."

Donovan's robe was wide open, exposing his beautifully sculpted chest. Dark gray briefs covered the dick that I'd enjoyed all night. The more I watched him, the more I was tempted to phone my boss and cash in one of my vacation days.

"Nonsense. Putting something quick in your body is a *no* from me," he said. "Let me feed you something good."

"Okay," I said, giving in quickly. Since I met him a year ago, my unhealthy eating habits had converted into better food choices. Choices my body thanked me for, inside and out.

"Return to me when you get off. I made reservations for us."

I spent more time at his home than my own. My spacious condo on the other side of the city was fully furnished. I'd paid a pretty penny for an interior decorator to take care of every inch of the glorious space for me.

Donovan's massive loft supplied a warm welcome. His King-sized bed embraced my body like I belonged in it.

The tall, white walls in his home were impossible to get bored of. They were endless and accompanied by fine pieces of black art. I loved spending time at his place.

"I always return to you, Donovan," I reminded him with an innocent smile attached. I bat my lashes to emphasize my teasing.

Donovan leaned in for a kiss as he flipped the omelet to its other side. I met him half-way, brushing my fingers through his thick beard as I indulged in him.

"I really have to get going, babe. It's Friday and traffic is going to be insane."

"I'll pack it to go for you," he insisted. There was no use in fighting him about it. He would win. And I gave in to his willingness to take care of me every time.

"Where did you make reservations for us?" I asked. It was worth a try. However, I anticipated the amused scoff that emitted from him.

"Now why would I let you in on that?" One of his bushy eyebrows rose. His caramel hue made me smile. I bit my bottom lip in awe, wishing I had extra time to feel him inside of me again.

"Because you love me?" I cooed. My inquiry was rhetorical, of course. Donovan's love and adoration for me spoke for itself.

Every delicate touch to my skin.

Every kiss on my sensitive neck.

Proven.

Donovan smirked and bypassed my question. While packing my breakfast to go, he licked his lips, then produced a slight head nod.

"You already know what it is." He stuffed Tupperware filled with fruit in my purple lunch bag. The spinach and Italian cheese omelet he made for me accompanied it. My stomach growled from the aroma of the green peppers and tomatoes he used.

"I can't wait to see you later," he said, pulling me close. Embracing me securely in his arms, he kissed my cheek and hung the long strap of my lunchbox over my shoulder.

"Ditto, handsome. Try enjoying your day off. That means don't stalk the camera feed at your restaurant. Relax and focus on yourself today. Trust your workers. For once," I said. "Promise me."

Donovan patted my ass and kept his hand at the small of my back until we reached the front door.

"I'll try my best."

"I'm serious, Donovan."

"Me too, woman." With his index finger, he lifted my chin and spoke against my lips. "Hurry back to me."

"I'll try my best."

Hiking my ankle-length skirt to my waist, he roamed underneath it. Donovan pushed my panties aside, rubbing my clit until the instant moisture that formed made him chuckle in my ear.

"Damn," he groaned.

"She always gets like that for you," I reminded him.

"And I'm always shocked." Removing his hand, he licked his fingers, then smashed his perfect, full lips into mine. "I love you, beautiful. Have a good day." Lowering my skirt, he smoothed it over my ass, patting it once more.

"I'll try my best," I repeated, serious this time. After biting his bottom lip, I kissed it to ease the pain before turning my back to him and reaching for the doorknob.

My full-on smile greeted the beaming sun when I opened the door. Donovan nestled his head against my neck, tickling me with his beard. I attempted to fight him off, but his hold on me was firm.

Strong and durable.

Just the way I liked it.

A pink Camry slammed on brakes in front of his abode, alongside the curb. Mirror tints concealed whoever was inside until a woman stepped out. She stomped up the steep, oval driveway and my giggles subsided with every step she took toward us. A conniving smile curled her pink, glossed lips as she approached us.

"Stay calm," he whispered in my ear and pulled me close to his side.

Immediately defensive, I straightened my posture and folded my arms across my chest.

"Cute," she reached us and said. The sun pinpointed the auburn highlights in her jet-black hair. A thick bun sat on top of her head, directly in the middle of it.

"What are you doing here, Veronica?"

Veronica

I'd heard her name enough times to know who she was. She was the woman who'd taken advantage of his kindness for three years. The woman who'd cheated on him countless times with an ex she refused to leave behind—an ex she claimed was *just a friend*.

From what I heard, the truth had come out during an egotistical match between her ex-boyfriend and Donovan. Donovan thought he had Veronica's heart, soul and body... until her ex outed their ongoing relations with each other.

"Now, is that any way to greet the love of your

7

life? Isn't that what you used to call me?" Veronica put her hand on her hip and stared up into his golden-brown eyes. Her light brown orbs focused intently on his until he pulled away from her to look at me.

"You trust me, right?" He gazed into my eyes until I managed a slow-motion nod.

"I do," I cleared my throat and said.

"Good." He kissed my forehead and guided me out the door. He pushed past Veronica to walk me to my car. "Don't be late to work on my behalf. I'll call you at your office when she leaves to tell you why she's here."

"Sure," I said and shrugged. I didn't have anything else to give. Nothing I could say to rewind time and lock us inside while Veronica knocked on the door until she comprehended the point to leave.

"Mona—"

"It's fine," I cut him off and disarmed my car alarm to get in. I would be safe behind the dark tint on my Volkswagen. My disappointment wouldn't be visible, nor would my insecurity of his ex arriving unexpectedly.

Donovan stepped back and brushed his hand down his dismayed face as I slammed my car door.

As if he could see me behind the dark tints, his eyes were locked on the window.

I wasn't mad at him.

I couldn't be.

Donovan hadn't done anything wrong.

I was mad at the woman from his past who'd resurfaced. And mad at the confusion that was unexpectedly thrown in our mix.

Why is she here?

She'd made her choice. Veronica had chosen another man over him. Her decision slapped him in the face, leaving him with a broken heart and trust issues that I'd helped him overcome. They'd been broken up for over two years. Their three-year relationship was in the past.

As I backed out of his driveway with hesitancy, I looked back and forth from the front door they'd entered and closed and the road. I missed him already, and I hated that he was with her.

Focusing on my tasks at the office was going to be impossible.

How did he expect me to focus knowing she was there with him, possibly drooling over who she'd betrayed and lost?

Impossible.

Until I heard from him and received an explanation for her arrival, I wouldn't be able to settle my fast-beating heart down. I wouldn't be able to focus amid my rapid thoughts.

It wasn't him I didn't trust, it was her.

"Now, is that any way to greet the love of your life?" she asked him.

Her inquiry triggered something within me. Actually, it triggered everything inside of me. I'd heard his deep baritone crack before. It happened during an explanation of their relationship's demise. I'd sat against the headboard countless nights—whether my headboard or his—holding Donovan in my arms while he tried to sort through his emotions. I'd listened to him vent about her in his most vulnerable state.

Suddenly, she was back, and it made me wonder...

Was he still in love with her? Was she still considered the love of his life?

My insecurities were rushing to the forefront. I'd begun to doubt everything we ever said to each other. Every caress and touch we shared with love in our bright eyes were in question, too.

From the rear-view mirror, a cop car with flashing lights was approaching quickly. My heart raced, threatening to collapse from the unnerving pressure of it all. Once the cop sped around me, a wave of relief washed over me.

The relief only lasted a second.

Obsessing over Donovan being alone with his ex came right back to taunt me.

The main thing on my mind was reaching my destination, so I could charge into my office and wait by the phone for his call.

I needed reassurance that Donovan's heart belonged to me.

Chapter 2

DONOVAN

My heart felt just as uneasy as Mona's body language was.

On the way to her car, her shoulders slouched. Her sweet voice weakened, becoming fainter with each additional word she spoke to me. After an uninterrupted night of making love to the woman of my dreams, the woman I'd previously assumed was the love of my life popped up at my front door.

Veronica had arrived unannounced and unwanted. She was as beautiful as I remembered, and more annoying than I recalled her being.

"Don't be late to work on my behalf. I'll call you at your office when she leaves to tell you why she's here." With my hand at the small of her back, I walked Mona to her cherry red Volkswagen.

I took it as a good sign that she let me touch her during such a trying time. I'd taken my time to learn every inch of her body. I studied my woman inside and out during the year we'd known each other, especially during the last six months we'd been exclusive.

Mona's blissful expression had transformed into a serious mug. Right now, I wasn't sure if she wanted to beat my ass or Veronica's.

Perhaps both.

"Sure," she said and shrugged.

She shrugged like it was nothing to her, but I knew the truth. This shit was bothering her more than it was screwing with my own head.

"Mona—" I tried to reason with her and give her the reassurance she needed. Her chocolate skin that usually radiated warmth was turning cold to my touch.

"It's fine," she cut me off and unlocked her car door to get inside. I stood outside of it frozen in place, contemplating my next move.

Snapping me out of my thoughts, Mona slammed her door. The tints on her car concealed her stunning identity, shutting me out. I stepped back and brushed my hand down my face.

Focused on her dark-tinted driver's window, I hoped like hell she noticed the sorrow in my eyes. I hoped she recognized the fucking stiffness taking over my limbs.

Mona backed out of the driveway slowly and I doubled-back to the front door reluctantly. Reluctant to let her go, yet ready to face Veronica to determine why she'd showed up.

I stormed inside my loft looking for her. She knew every inch of it. She was probably more familiar with the tall walls than I was. Veronica's editorial career gave her the luxury of working from home. Wherever she found comfort, she settled in and got down to business for her clients. I'd watched her plop down in specific corners of my loft many days. With her back against the cold wall, she always sat Indian-style with a satisfied smile on her face. Veronica lived for her career. It had come before me many times, and I was okay with that.

"*Whatever makes you happy,*" I always reminded her.

"Veronica," I huffed when I found her lying across my bed.

Mona's signature vanilla scent lingered in the

air. Her very being was taking over my space little by little, and I didn't mind it. I welcomed it.

Veronica stood from the bed to approach me. "She's pretty," she said, concluding her statement with a shrug.

"She's beautiful," I corrected her.

If we were being precise, then I should've included that Mona was fucking stunning. I should've mentioned how lost I got whenever I admired her deep melanin for too long. The detail I could dig deep into on how her brown eyes stood out against her chocolate skin would take all day. I would've concluded with how much I loved it when she wore light colors. I preferred holding her warm, naked body in my arms above anything else, but light colors covering her skin were a beautiful second place prize.

"But I know you didn't come here to give out compliments," I said.

"I didn't," she agreed and laughed down at her feet.

"Why are you here, Veronica?"

"I miss you, okay? Is that such a crime?"

"After all the hard work you put in to ruin us…" I paused to chuckle. "It should be."

"I thought you would've moved out by now."

Dropping her hair from its bun, she held her head back and shook it from side to side until her hair flowed beyond her shoulders. Roaming her fingers through it, she stopped in front of me before seductively tucking a strand behind her ear. The little things she used to do always got a rise out of me. I never thought I would see the day her beauty wouldn't impact me anymore.

The day had come, and those other days were long gone.

"I'm not in a rush anymore." I stepped back and glared at her.

The hard feelings I had toward her had diminished over time, but the truth remained. She'd crossed me in the worst possible way. She'd given herself to another man while I was committed to her.

Veronica was untrue to me.

The pussy she promised belonged to me whenever I was deep inside of her had been promised to another man, too. A man she claimed was her best friend.

Typical.

"I guess that means I was the rush," she said, putting two and two together.

"You guess?" I scoffed. She knew damn well she

was the rush. Veronica had become fire under my ass since the day I met her. Everything she ever mentioned she wanted, I tried my hardest to give her.

A big, two-story house.

A ring.

A family.

It was all attainable, and I was willing to jump head first into everything with her. Then, her true colors and infidelity came blasting through, full force.

"Donovan, I need to apologize."

"You don't need to." I caught her wrist before she reached up and touched my face. "I moved on without it. I don't need it now."

"I realize what I did hurt you and I'm—" She stopped talking when I burst out laughing.

I didn't want to hear that shit. She was only able to stand in front of me right now because of how much I once loved her. Veronica was only able to enter my space again because of our history together. Fronting like she never meant anything to me would be fraud on my behalf. I would always care about her.

Still, I didn't want to hear that shit.

"Are you done?" I asked, motioning toward the threshold.

Ready to push her out of the front door, I moved around her to lead the way.

"Is this thing between you and her—"

"*Serious?*" I looked back and rose an eyebrow, side-eyeing her. "It is," I answered. "Very serious."

"And you're sure it isn't because we... I mean, because I... ruined us?"

"Veronica." I dropped my head and repressed my laughter. A part of me wanted to laugh in her face.

A big part of me.

My parents raised me better than that. Despite how much she fucked me over, I would continue to treat Veronica with respect.

"I *am* with her because you ruined us."

The gleam in her eyes reminded me of how selfish she was. After everything she'd done, she returned with hope that I'd forgiven her. She probably assumed I would drop everything to be with her again.

"Thank God you did, you know? Ruin everything, that is. I would've never met Mona. She's everything I've ever wanted. Everything I never knew I needed," I clarified. "Most of all, she's selfless. You wouldn't know much about that, would you?"

Seeing her cry used to break me down. Whenever Veronica was hurt by anyone or anything, it brought me to my knees. She was standing before me with tears cascading down her light brown cheeks, and I felt nothing. I only wanted her to leave so I could phone Mona right-away and hear her sweet voice again.

I was anxious to tell her we were good. That we would always be good! I was anxious to remind her that our connection was solid, and to tell her I couldn't wait to hold her in my arms when she returned to me.

"That's not fair," she said.

"Let me see you out." I put my hand on her back and led her to the front door.

I had energy to debate her sentiments. A lot of it! Given my position, I had the right to carry on about our demise and how she was the major cause of it. Instead, I decided to conserve my energy for something better.

Veronica didn't deserve it.

———

MY HOMEBOY AND BUSINESS PARTNER, GRAYSON, checked me the ball, then dropped his head and sighed. "Hold on. Run that by me again," he said.

I chuckled because I knew he'd heard me loud and clear the first time. He'd listened carefully as I described Veronica's unexpected pop-up to him.

If anyone knew and understood the full story on us, it was him.

Grayson and I had been thick as thieves since our freshman year in high school. I trusted him with my life and my business—personally and financially. As an only child, he was the closest thing I ever had to an older brother.

My parents treated him as such, too. And strangers assumed he was my brother because we resembled each other in looks.

"Please don't make me rehash that shit, bro."

He caught the ball I aimed at his chest, then dribbled it beside him. We were the only duo on the large basketball court in Grayson's suburban neighborhood. The community was always quiet, peaceful and engulfed with elders walking their small, colorful dogs. I clowned him often about living in a retirement community. I wondered how he pulled that shit off.

"Not all of it. Just the part before she walked out the door to leave. What's that bullshit she said?"

"She said she's willing to fight for me," I repeated. That was the same part that blew my mind, too. Veronica didn't attempt to fight for me, or us, when we were together. She surrendered the moment she contemplated giving herself to another man.

"That's it. That's the bullshit I'm talking about. How'd you respond to that?"

"I closed the door on her, man. I tried to call Mona afterward to explain everything to her, but she isn't feeling me right now. She didn't answer my call."

Grayson shot the ball and missed. He scoffed as it bounced off the rim and rolled back over to him. "You know I gotta keep it G with you, right?" Grayson attempted another shot. This time, he made it.

"Yeah. I was waiting on it."

"The fuck were you thinking? Sending your woman off to chop it up with your ex? You're too old not to know better, Don. Too experienced not to play your cards right."

"I didn't send her off, G. She was headed to work. I didn't want her to be late."

"Do women think with logic or emotion, bro? You should've hit Fraudonica with the, *whatever you need to say to me, you can say it in front of us,* line," he said. "Trust me, Mona would've appreciated that shit."

I brushed my hand down my face, smoothing it over my beard.

Grayson was right. I did know better.

If I was eighteen again, I would've come up with some narcissistic reason to justify my actions. But I'd grown. After a decade of coming into my own, I should've known better. Should've done better.

"Damn." I huffed.

"You feel it now, huh?" Grayson laughed.

"I fucked up," I mumbled to myself.

"You fucked up," he agreed, nodding vigorously. He wasn't cutting me any slack over my incompetence. "Now you gotta kiss ass all night. Sucks for you."

Grayson twirled the basketball ball on his index finger while he mocked me. Utilizing my being distracted, he dribbled the ball between his legs, then double-crossed me to jog down the court and dunk the ball.

"Show off." I scoffed. He'd always been better than me at ball.

Jogging back up the court, he tossed the ball at me. My reflexes caught on and grabbed it before my attention did.

"Does your love for Mona exceed what you felt for Fraudonica?" he asked.

I smirked at the thought of Mona. If only I could put into words how I felt about her.

"G, I thought I had it right before, but. I know I have it right now."

"When you know, you know, bro. Hold on to that."

Grayson and I usually discussed business pertaining to our restaurant when we met up at the court, but I couldn't wrap my head around anything else besides fixing things with Mona.

G part-owned both of our locations in Louisville and Lexington. He knew the ins and outs of the food business, and he interacted with our management team more than I did. I figured if he had something important to spill, he would've done it by now.

In the meantime, I was focused on ways to *kiss ass* all night. Whatever it took to assure Mona she was the only one for me.

Chapter 3
MONA

Conflicted at an intersection, I glanced in my rearview mirror to make sure no one was impatiently waiting behind me.

Left, or right?

Turning right would lead me home to my condo, and I wasn't completely sure if that was where I wanted to be. After a rough day at the office, I wanted Donovan more than ever. I'd sat behind my desk, confined within the four, pastel pink walls for ten torturous hours.

I hadn't accepted his calls all day because I couldn't wrap my head around the sudden visit from his ex. I'd gone from needing to know why Veronica showed face to feeling nervous about the reason behind her visit overall.

At this point, I didn't care anymore. I wanted him. I needed to return to him before missing him became unbearable.

Who knew how I would react when that happened!

Finally, I took a sharp turn after someone behind me laid down on their horn.

Left, it is.

My heart was leading me to its rightful owner. Whatever he needed to say to me, or wanted to explain over the phone would now have to be a face to face discussion. Besides, I preferred staring in his mesmerizing orbs whenever he spoke to me anyway.

His eyes always revealed the truth. If he bull-shitted me about anything, I could discern the truth through his eyes. I'd mastered getting to know them. When they bounced over me, he missed me. When they were still and glossy, he was vulnerable and needed me most in that moment. His eyes showcased every emotion he ever tried to hold back from me.

The drive to Donovan's loft was thirty minutes away from my office. My playlist of soft R&B wasn't helping my case. One of the thousand songs we'd deemed ours cooed through the speakers of my car like an entrancing melody.

The jazz sequence on Masego's, *Tadow*, track soothed my soul every time I heard it. It took me back to the first time Donovan made love to me. A soft jazz assortment played in the background as my moans coincided with the music.

To be skin to skin with him was a privilege I wasn't willing to hand over to any woman.

Gripping the steering wheel harder, I made my way to him by driving five miles over the speed limit. I couldn't wait to be in his arms again, enveloped in his magnetic embrace.

Surprisingly, traffic this Friday evening wasn't that bad. The streets weren't congested, allowing me to switch lanes and reach my destination quicker than the half-hour it usually took me to arrive.

His Charger was parked at the top of his wide, curved driveway. Pulling in behind it, I cut off my car and sat behind the wheel for a moment, reflecting on what I would say when he opened the door.

I'd ignored his calls to ponder my own assumptions about the sudden visit from his ex. Lost in my own head, I hadn't bothered to talk to him for ten long hours.

I snatched my purse from the passenger's seat

and stepped out of my car. I cringed at the loud alarm when I pressed my key fob. Between the cameras outside of his home and my car alarm, he knew I'd returned to him.

I found Donovan leaning against the threshold when I made it to the front door. Instant chemistry was known to be dangerous, and I'd been afraid of him and his potential to ruin me since the first time I laid eyes on him.

Donovan's height of six-five was the first thing that initially captured my attention. His long, bow-legs contained sex appeal all on their own. I'd entered Powell's Southern Smokehouse on Main Street with eyes bigger than my rumbling stomach. On that day, I had no idea I would leave fulfilled with more than just amazing barbecue ribs. I'd gotten me, and my two older sisters who accompanied me, a free meal. Best of all, I'd gotten the owner's number.

History from there!

"I'm sorry I'm late," I said. "Long day at work. Can we still make the reservations?"

Donovan didn't speak. Reaching for my hand, he pulled me inside, then secured the locks on the door behind me. He hung my purse on the coat rack beside the door and led me into his bedroom without a word. His grip on me was tight and the first sign of how much he'd missed me.

Inside of his bedroom, a trail of rose petals led to his master bathroom. I looked up at his handsome face and blushed. My cheeks were warm, temperature rising due to his charismatic thoughtfulness. I admired how effortless it was for him to woo me. For him to swoon me.

He pushed the door to his bathroom open, nodding for me to enter. Bubbles topped the steaming water in the widespread, oval tub. Additional rose petals decorated the edge of the tub, some floating on top of the glistening bubbles.

"Donovan Powell," I whispered in awe. After the day I had—on top of overthinking the visit from his ex—this was just what I needed.

"I wasn't sure you would return to me after this morning, but I hoped and prayed you would," he said.

Donovan pushed my hair aside to kiss the back of my neck. He removed my necklace, followed by every accessory on me. Slowly, he stripped me bare. While cupping my breasts in his large hands, he leaned down to kiss my forehead. Like my body was a maze to him, he observed me like he didn't know where to start. Donovan stared at me like my body was a wonderland he'd never explored.

"Get in. I'll bring you a glass of your favorite wine in a few minutes. Dinner is in the oven. Don't sweat the reservations."

"Donovan..." I called out to him before he exited. I needed to apologize. I'd handled things all wrong by ignoring him. I reminded him countless times that I trusted him with everything inside of me. My actions went against that claim.

"We'll talk about it later," he said and walked out.

He'd left me to it, and I wasted no time settling inside the warm bath to wash the day away.

What a day.

———

"TELL ME ABOUT YOUR DAY," HE SAID. AS IF HIS touch hadn't already gotten my juices flowing, his deep resound surely did the trick.

While sitting on his bed in a towel, I tightened the other towel around my damp hair, then smiled as he dropped to his knees in front of me. He had my Winter Candy Apple lotion from Bath and Body Works in his hand.

My favorite!

Whenever it went on sale for a limited time during the holiday season, I purchased it in bulk, making sure I never ran out.

Once his firm hands covered my feet, I moaned with relief. Donovan lathered the lotion over my feet and legs. One at a time, he focused attentively on a tense area, massaging his fingers deeply into my skin until the body lotion vanished. I was sad every time it did.

"I don't hear you," he said.

"Oh," I whispered, snapping out of the trance I was under. "It was eventful, to say the least." I sighed. "No. That's the wrong word. It was hectic. Mr. Loomis took the day off."

"Your boss? I thought you liked when he took the day off."

"Usually, I do. I love when he's out of my face. But today, he called the shots from home. It was worse than when he's actually there. I imagine that's how your management team feels about you sometimes."

"Hey. This doesn't have anything to do with me." He chuckled. "I took your advice and left business alone all day. I even shot some hoops with G."

"I'm happy to hear that. How is he?"

"He's good. He told me to tell you he said hey."

I'd only met Grayson in passing a few times, but he was nice. I'd deemed him a smooth player when he took my hand in his, kissed it, and then introduced himself as Donovan's brother. I could tell he was a headache for more than one woman by that gesture alone.

I'd lost my train of thought when Donovan moved upward to moisturize my thighs. My body reacted to him without hesitation. Leaning back on my elbows, I sighed pleasurably as he pressed his thumbs in my skin. He was amazing with his hands.

"I know I'm just a financial advisor, but—"

"No, baby. You're *thee* financial advisor," he corrected me.

"I am, huh?" I reached forward to rub his head. No matter how small or unimportant I felt amongst my peers sometimes, Donovan made sure to gas me up. He uplifted me before my ass could ever hit the ground.

"Damn right. Don't you forget it."

"Donovan..." I whispered. He stood at the sound of his name. Towering over me, he looked down at me like he knew it was time. Time to discuss *her* and why she'd come here.

"Why didn't you answer or return my calls earlier, Mona?"

"I'm sorry."

"Don't be. Tell me why you ignored me."

"I guess I was reluctant to hear the reason why she was here."

"But you're not anymore?"

"A little bit. I just need to know."

"She came here to apologize," he said, sitting next to me. Pulling me onto his lap, he secured me in his arms and slanted his eyes at my blank facial expression. My lips were sealed. I had no idea what to say about that.

"She said a lot of things I don't care to repeat. Her feelings don't mean anything to me anymore. I agreed to hear her out because I thought something was wrong, but even that isn't my responsibility anymore. I'm no longer the man who's interested in loving or saving her. I'm no longer the man who wants anything to do with her. Her unexpected visit further proved that truth to me."

My silence didn't bother him but avoiding eye contact did. He made me face him by griping my chin and turning my head toward him.

"What do you want out of this, Mona? I failed

to ask the last woman what she wanted. I assumed it was a life with me until she fucked me over."

"I don't ask for much, Donovan. I only want to love you."

"And what do you want from me?"

"For you to get to know me like no man has ever known me. Learn to love me like no man has ever loved me. But I won't ever battle another woman for your heart. I'm a strong woman, but I don't have the strength for that fight."

"No one is asking you to fight for me. You're so blinded by her resurfacing that you can't see I've already chosen you. You're it for me."

"Isn't *she* the first woman you truly loved?"

"I loved her, yes. That's what it was," he said. "You and I are what's happening right now. This." He pointed between us. "This is what it is. What does that have to do with us?"

"Nothing," I whispered, eyes locked on his lips. "Can we kiss and make up already?"

"Na. I'm good. You played me all day. You don't fuck with me."

"I already apologized." I kissed his cheek. I rubbed my fingers through his beard before pressing my lips firmly against his. "Forgive me?" I performed a pout he couldn't resist. Donovan could never bypass a pair of sad eyes from me.

"Before the night is out," he said. "You hungry?"

"Yes."

"Me too." Removing me from his lap, he tossed me onto the bed and snatched the towel from around me. I clasped my legs shut until he motioned for me to open them with a head nod.

Donovan looked at me like I was the only woman he ever loved. He would never understand how much that guise from him meant to me.

He kissed from my lips to the top of my thighs, and I moaned the moment his tongue grazed my inner thigh. A tongue kiss to my clit had me apologizing for ignoring his calls earlier.

"I love you," he mumbled against my clit.

He pleased me better than any man had ever pleased me.

"I love you too, baby."

————

IN THE MIDDLE OF THE NIGHT, MY GROWLING stomach disturbed my peaceful slumber. While comfortable in his arms, my head rested on his chest until my eyes popped open. My body was fed up with me. Donovan's dick wasn't the only nourishment I needed.

After I managed to slip from underneath his arm that was wrapped around me, I planted a soft kiss on his chest, then climbed out of bed and headed straight for the kitchen. I was excited to see what he'd cooked for us. Though we hadn't made it that far, I knew he'd gone all out for me. He always did—especially where cooking was concerned.

Making my way through the darkness in his loft was like a stroll through the park on a bright and sunny day. I knew his home well. At the drop of a dime, I could visualize every part of it.

The subtle light over the kitchen stove greeted me at the same time I stepped onto the cold, wooden floor. It was enough light for me to open the stove and carefully pull the contents from it.

"My favorite," I whispered, licking my lips.

His famous three-cheese, beef lasagna was stacked beautifully in a deep, glass dish. The cheese and meat layers looked delicious. My stomach growled louder as I admired the masterly appearance he took so much pride in.

As I cut a small section from the corner of the dish, I sensed him. Frozen in place, my eyes were locked on the lasagna in front of me until he spoke and pulled me from the spell of his hypnotizing presence.

"You got me, too?" he asked from the opposite side of the kitchen. Slowly but surely, he made his way to me. I took a deep breath when his warm hard-on pressed against my ass.

We were both bare and naked as the day we were born. Truth be told, it was the way we preferred each other.

"Yes. I'll fix enough for us to share." I leaned back to feel more of him. With him, it was impossible to get enough. I closed my eyes and smiled when he kissed my cheek.

You were a lucky woman if you were loved by Donovan Powell.

How could anyone before me fuck that up?

Although I would never understand it, luckily for me they had ruined it for themselves. I had him now, and his love was one of the best things that ever happened to me.

"Can I ask you something?" I turned around to face him.

"Anything." He nodded. Dodging his kiss, I placed my hand over his mouth and laughed.

"What do you want out of this? I know we've

only known each other for a year. And we've only spent six months of that time loving each other beyond anything we've ever imagined. Is this... are we..." I stalled, struggling to find the right words.

Removing my hand from his mouth, he kissed the top of it and said, "Mona, I want a love that stays. Something strong and permanent in a temporary world. I want a love that hovers when we're gone. Something our children will look up to and refuse to settle for anything less than. I want a kind soul. To fall asleep and wake up knowing I'm safe as a man—that my manhood is always intact—always protected. I get all that with you. I want you."

I wasn't breathing.

I couldn't.

All I could do was stare into his loving eyes that longed for me.

Reaching up to rub his handsome face, I exhaled deeply, then dropped my head the moment a tear cascaded down my cheek.

"What's that about?" He lifted my chin with a finger, kissing my tears away.

"I've been hurt too, Donovan. More times than I'm willing to admit. I've been stupid for a few men, assuming my love could change them. I thought I could love hard and forgive their wrongdoings until they finally noticed what they had in me. Eventually, I got tired. I said I was done with love. Told myself I was done trying to achieve a happily ever after... until I met you."

"You're scared?" he asked. "Scared I'll hurt you?"

"Sometimes. Most of all, I'm scared to lose you."

"We have a long way to go, beautiful. I'm grateful for that. Plenty of time to show you better than I could ever tell you."

More time with him was the ultimate gift, but if it turned out to be endless, my heart would remain complete.

"No, no, no, no." I tried to stop him before he lifted me off my feet and wrapped my legs around his waist. "Donovan," I whispered.

His dick was at my entrance. He was smoother than I considered. More skillful than I comprehended in that moment until he entered me with ease.

"Don," I moaned. Wrapping my arms around his neck, I held onto him for dear life. I doubted he would ever drop me, but holding him close felt good. Sensational, even.

Entangling his fingers in my hair, he pulled my

head back to kiss my neck. "Breaking your heart isn't in the cards for me, Mona."

As he carried me back to his bedroom, I bounced on his dick and whimpered in his ear. I wondered if we would ever find time to eat.

Donovan laid me down on the bed. He was always exceptionally gentle, like he was afraid he would break me in half if he did too much. It was like that until he got into his groove. Once his strokes turned aggressive, his large hand engulfed my neck and he aired apologies in my ear while fucking me senseless.

"Deeper," I moaned in the heat of the moment.

The nerve of me! Asking for more when I could hardly handle the thick inches of dick he was already giving me.

I parted my thighs wider to welcome all of him. My mouth was dry as I gasped for air. My heart raced as I dug my nails in his back and pleaded for mercy.

"Recite it to me," he instructed. His baritone had gotten deeper. I knew it was a demand. "I want to hear it while you come for me."

He had to be out of his mind.

This was a first—a first that stumped me until he repeated his request with a threat.

"I'm not going to ask you again."

"You felt familiar the moment I met you," I started. Donovan would never forget the poetry piece I read to him the night I confessed I'd fallen in love with him. Word for word, he recollected the art written by Beau Taplin entitled, *Deja Vu.*

It was a part of my heart. If my soul could speak to him, the very words would swarm him.

"A lovely sort of Déjà Vu." I wrapped my thighs around him tighter. *"When we spoke, or laughed, or danced, I became overwhelmed by the powerful sensation that I had been here before."*

My thighs trembled, body on the verge of convulsing.

"And when we kissed, I felt the energies of a thousand lives on our lips..." Donovan interrupted me with a passionate kiss. I moaned in his mouth as my body exploded.

When my eyes closed, I spotted colorful fireworks erupt. We whispered each other's names, then panted as we struggled to catch our breath.

"Like our souls had known each other all along," I concluded the poem and snuggled against him.

I wasted no time drifting off to sleep to fast forward to the next day. Another day with him, was another day well spent.

I DESERVED DONOVAN POWELL.

All of him.

Every unique trait associated with him.

Every inch of his beautiful, mouth-watering shaft.

He stared at my lips as I complained about having spent another work day away from him, and also as I spoke about my sisters, my job, bills and anything else that came to mind.

Donovan nodded frequently, listening observantly as he massaged his fingers into my skin. He rubbed my feet like I'd been on them all day. But that's how the heels I wore to work made me feel, anyway. On the opposite end of the couch, he lounged with my feet on his lap while laughing hard at parts of my banter like I was a comedian.

"Enough about me." I scooted to the middle cushion to get closer to him—to inhale his natural, captivating scent.

"*More* about you," he countered, pulling me onto his lap.

I laid my head on his shoulder. "You don't get tired of hearing me ramble about nothing when I get home from work?"

"I'll never get tired of hearing you ramble."

It was unreal how sweet he was to me—how sweet he'd always been to me.

It never diminished.

It didn't fluctuate.

It only broadened and got better with time.

"We always go into detail on what happened in my last relationship. What about yours?" he asked, totally catching me off-guard. My eyes widened as I pondered his question.

My previous relationships were the last things I wanted to discuss. Donovan thought he was fooled by his ex. *Man!* He had no idea how I'd played the fool for many of mine multiple times.

"I... it was..." I paused to shake my head. "There were many of them. I was a serial dater, if you can call it that." I dropped my head and judged myself. It sounded much worse admitting it out loud. "I mean, I didn't have sex with all of them." Donovan lifted my head by placing an index finger under my chin.

"No one here is judging you, woman. I have no rights to that. Don't do that to yourself."

I took a deep breath, exhaling deeply before I spoke again. "I guess I was looking for something in them. Well, I know I was. But I never found it. Ever.

And whenever I took it too far by trying to wait it out, it failed tremendously, because I was looking for something…"

"Then, I found you," he said.

"Yes. Right after I stopped looking and focused on myself… you found me, and I finally found *it*. I have everything I've always wanted in you."

Donovan cupped the side of my face, displaying a sexy half-smile. "Thank God it never worked with anyone else."

"Thank God." I swallowed hard with tears welling in my eyes.

"I love you, Mona."

"I love you too, Donovan. So much."

"Come here," his voice aired deep—so deep that the pearl between my legs ached.

My body knew when it was time.

Time to enjoy him sexually.

Time to relish in an intimacy that took my breath away.

"I'm here," I said, straddling his lap.

My heart banged against my chest. Donovan didn't feel too good to be true; I knew he was real. Every bit of real that it scared me sometimes. My submission to him made me feel physically weak.

"Tell me again." He smiled.

That handsome, blinding, beautiful ass smile.

He thought he was slick! And he was.

Going into my shorts, he pulled my panties aside to rub my clit.

"Donovan." I panted.

Coaching me to relax, he instructed me to lie my head on his shoulder. To grind on his fingers until a powerful climax ripped through my body.

"Tell me again," he repeated, holding me closely. My thighs trembled, breath picking up as I tried my hardest to pace myself.

"I love you," I whispered against his lips. "You felt familiar the moment I met…" I began to recite our favorite piece. "A lovely sort of…" I squealed during an explosive climax, unable to complete the poem most significant to us.

"I love you too, beautiful." He removed his hand from my shorts and licked my juices from his fingers.

"Thank God you're here," I said.

ne week later...

It was only noon and there was only one corner booth available in the Smokehouse.

Large groups of patrons hung out near the entrance, some even lingering outside the restaurant with a pager in hand, waiting for their turn to dine.

I entered with a pep in my step and a sly smile on my face. I hated that they had to wait to dine, but I appreciated the business because it wasn't always this way.

After stepping out on faith four years ago, I opened the first location for Powell's Southern Smokehouse in my hometown.

It had been a long time coming.

I spent agonizing years in school earning a Business Management degree. I racked up over eighty thousand dollars in student loan debt while attending the University of Louisville. After all that, graduating wasn't even the real plug toward my opening. The journey to opening a restaurant included tedious steps that almost counted me out, but I persisted. My parents and Grayson made sure of it.

The inside of the Smokehouse used to be dead. I was lucky if ten people dined within the twelve hours we were open. At one point, I put more money into the business than I ever believed I would get back.

God had a funny way of psyching His children out. Just when I thought I was down and out and wasting my time, business picked up. An everlasting wave of consumers started visiting our establishment like they'd been summoned.

Grayson probably had something to do with it. He'd always been the mastermind of our two-man crew. G knew how to make shit happen. Regardless of how the rise in our business occurred, I was grateful for it.

"I'm glad you strolled in this muthafucka cheesin' n'shit. One of us needs to be in a good mood," Grayson greeted me. Without knocking, I'd barged into his office showcasing my good mood.

"What's your problem?" I plopped down on one of the high-back chairs in front of his desk. "Business is booming. Numbers are more than good. Life is *good*!"

"Loverboy." He scoffed and looked up from his desk to side-eye me. I only chuckled, unable to debate him on that.

Inside, I was hype and acting like a fool in love from the high I was on. Mona's love had me that way. I couldn't front on how good she made me feel. We gotten closer after my ex popped up unannounced. I wanted to thank Veronica for that. If her goal was to cause confusion, she failed. She'd done the exact opposite.

On the outside, though, I had to chill and protect my manhood. I couldn't be out here skipping around and off my game because her love felt too good to be true. I needed to focus, but damn she had me wide open.

"Business is in fact booming," he confirmed while aggressively tapping the keys on his MacBook. "Numbers are better than ever, too," he concluded.

"But?" I wondered out loud, ready for the bad news he was bound to drop on me.

"*But...* our management team is full of idiots. They lack control over the other employees. They're fucking up their own bonus with food costs, which ultimately digs into our pockets. The Lexington location is thriving in these areas. Meanwhile, our first baby is mediocre. I'm salty about that."

"G." I brushed my hand down my face. "I hate to break it to you. I know how much you hate when I throw shit in your face. But you hired them. You promoted them to higher positions. You trained them, dawg."

"Man." He kissed his teeth. "I knew I would be wasting my time if I kicked it to you. Yo ass ain't no help."

"Handle that." I stood from my seat and rushed out of his office before he could get another word in. I couldn't let him fuck up my high. I hadn't been this high up since the last time I smoked the strongest grain of sativa in college.

Mona was a drug on her own. I was certain I would never be able to quit her. There wasn't a remedy available to help me with my addiction to her.

"What's up, boss?" one of our chefs greeted me the second I stepped foot in their area. My cooks worked their asses off to impress me, and sometimes overtime to prove how serious they took their craft.

Aside from the business aspect of things, cooking was my first love. My father had placed me alongside him in the kitchen at nine-years-old. Since then, the kitchen had been my refuge—my creative space to do what I did best. I wanted to employ a number of people who felt the same way. If cooking wasn't their passion, they couldn't work for me.

"Everything is everything, Des. You good?" I looked over his shoulder, impressed. "Your meal presentation gets better and better."

"I appreciate it, boss. I work on it when I'm at the crib, too," he said.

"Keep that up." I nodded, satisfied with his work ethic.

I was overdue for choosing a head chef. Desmond had been working hard for that title for months. The position was his, but I let him sweat it out. His hunger for the position made him work hard at all times.

"Stop by my office after your shift. I got good news for you," I informed him. After chopping it up with the other cooks, I headed out.

I was done prolonging Desmond's promotion. It was time. In addition, I was in a good mood. A mood patient enough to wait around while he filled out the proper paperwork for his new position.

Mona was responsible for my good mood and new-found patience.

———

BARGING INTO MY OFFICE SHORTLY AFTER I LEFT HIS, Grayson returned the favor of trying to irritate the hell out of me.

"I'm about to fuck up your day." He shook his head, closing the door behind him.

"I doubt it," I said. Everything was everything for me. My mood was too elevated to be knocked down. "Go ahead and tell me you fired one of my favorite employees."

"Na. That ain't it, chief." He dropped his head. "I wish it was something that easy to drop on you."

"You fucked up the budget?" I asked, starting to think the worst. Beads of sweat formed on his forehead as his dark brown skin flushed out on me.

Placing the back of his hand against his forehead, he sucked in a deep breath and said, "Fraudonica is here."

"You bullshitting?" I shot back, but his silence confirmed he was telling the truth.

"Did she request a table?" I asked.

"She's waiting on one," he said. "And she asked to speak with you."

"I'm not here."

"I tried that. She already peeped your car in the parking lot."

"I'm busy."

"I mentioned that too. She said she'll wait on you *and* the table. She got a friend with her. They're out there giggling and talking shit."

"I'm sure that's her meddling ass sister. She doesn't have any friends." I stood and huffed. "Call the police."

"C'mon, fam." Grayson chuckled. "I'm trying to stop her from blowing our spot up and that's what you come up with?"

"Shit." I shrugged. "I don't want to deal with her. Let them handle it. She's trespassing."

"That would've worked if you set that order up long ago."

I wish I had set that order up. I'd never taken Veronica for the crazy type. She changed faces after I moved on.

"I'll handle it," I said. Grayson blocked the

door, stopping me from leaving to confront her. "Move, man. What's up with you?"

"There's more." He brushed his hand down his face. "Your girl is here, too."

I kissed my teeth. "Now I know you fucking with me." I pushed him aside to witness the truth for myself. My luck couldn't have been that bad.

My woman and my ex woman in the same building? In my restaurant?

God must've been too busy to cut me any slack today.

Grayson followed closely behind me like we were headed to fight a gang of men. Similar situations never fazed him when he was in my position. He was a ladies man through and through. The slew of women who dealt with him knew his intentions. But this was out of the ordinary for me. I was a one woman's man. Mona's man, specifically. Veronica was trying to ruin that for me.

My strides were long and quick. The quicker I reached Mona, the better. My heart raced with each step, threatening to burst out of my damn chest. I'd never been a victim of anxiety until now. The surge of emotions that attacked me made me feel powerless in my own establishment.

"Has she been seated?" I questioned Grayson

about Mona.

"Yeah. Her and her sisters have already been seated."

"Fuck," I spat under my breath. "Her sisters are with her."

"Is that bad?"

"Just watch my back," I advised him.

At all times, Mona remained a calm woman. If she ever turned up, a whisper in her ear settled her down, and a kiss on her cheek took her breath away. Around her sisters, she was a different woman.

Mona's sisters were her biggest cheerleaders. She could go from zero to one-hundred in a matter of seconds with their encouragement and banter backing her up. Together, the Hill sisters were a dynamic force to be reckoned with. You couldn't tell them anything or stop them from defending themselves or each other if they felt disrespected in any way.

Though I wanted to keep Mona calm, I had to admit that my dick jumped whenever she showed out.

"I got you," Grayson said.

My first line of duty was escorting Veronica out of the Smokehouse before the calm increased to a storm.

Chapter 5

MONA

After we were seated in a booth at Powell's Southern Smokehouse, my sisters stared at me with goofy smiles on their faces. I rolled my eyes at their wisecracks.

Molli and Monika sat across from me, batting their eyelashes between giggles.

"What's that line Plies said again? *That lil coochie got some power!*" Monika deepened her tone to imitate the rapper's voice. "Being Donovan's girl-friend comes with perks, I see."

"Monika." I sighed. Molli egged her on by laughing loud and obnoxiously.

"The hostess said it would be a two-hour wait, then that fine chocolate man stepped in and seated us," Molli said. "You got some pull."

"That's Grayson," I explained. "He's Donovan's best friend and business partner."

"I don't care who he is to Donovan. Who can he be to me? Is he single?" Molli fanned herself with a menu. "Those light brown eyes. Pearly white teeth. Long bowlegs." Her fanning motion picked up as she carried on. "That dick print in them slacks!"

"I hate to break it to you, but he's a whore. A male whore," I said.

Grayson had always been respectful to me. And he was certainly a smart and handsome man. But I knew enough to determine him a player who got around. I'd unashamedly eavesdropped on enough of him and Donovan's conversations to discover the truth on why a good-looking man of his caliber was single.

"Ouch," Monika quipped.

"Right." Molli kissed her teeth. "Why he gotta be all that?"

"I'm just telling you what I know." I shrugged. "But yes, he's single."

"Good D usually comes with complications," Monika added. Molli and I snapped our necks in her in direction, staring her upside her head.

"How would you know? Let me guess. The dick

you've been stuck on since your junior year in high school came with a lot of complications?" Molli scoffed. "Mona, why do we hang out with married women?"

Our older sister, Monika, was happily married to her high school sweetheart. We'd never recalled a time they weren't happy with each other. They hardly argued and neither of them seemed to want any children.

At thirty-two-years-old, they were solely focused on each other. Their lives revolved around one another, and they preferred it that way.

"Complications, huh?" I side-eyed her.

"You two are ridiculous." She laughed. "Complications come in many forms. Don't let me and Joe fool you."

Suddenly, I zoned out. Their banter was silenced at the sight of Donovan. He'd stormed to the front of the restaurant with Grayson lingering closely behind.

My world always stopped when Donovan came into view. The moment I initially spotted him, I deemed him the finest man I ever laid eyes on in my twenty-seven years of living. Taking him in was a task. A breathtaking task that I would never grow tired of.

"No fucking way," I whispered, and my sisters turned around to follow my gaze.

"Who's that?" they questioned in unison. Molli squinted her eyes in their direction, probably frisking Grayson from head to toe.

"Who are those women they're talking to?" Monika looked back and forth from me to them.

My blood boiled when I recognized who *she* was. And I knew once my sisters discovered who she was they weren't going to help my annoyance with her subside. I'd vented to them on Group FaceTime once too many times. Her last visit was still fresh; her disrespect was still weighing heavy on my mind.

And there she was.

Again.

Standing in front of my man with a confident smile on her face.

Again.

"The one in the white tank-top is Veronica. I don't know who her friend is."

"What the hell is she doing here?" Molli nearly shouted.

"I don't know." I huffed. My eyes were set on Donovan. His jawline was clenched and one of his fists were balled as he brushed his other hand down his face.

"He's telling her to leave," Monika said.

"How do you know what he's telling her?" Molli spat.

The crazy middle child, Molli was. Our parents let her get away with it all her life. They blamed her theatrics on *Middle Child Syndrome*, claiming she acted like that because she didn't receive enough attention from them when we were children.

Molli used to joke that she would calm down when her twenties were behind her. But nope! She was a month away from her thirty-first birthday and she was still over the top.

Over the top *and* crazy!

"I read his lips," Monika tried to reason, but Molli wasn't the one who needed to be convinced. I didn't doubt Donovan told her to leave. I doubted she would.

Beyond my own security, Donovan made sure I was comfortable and understood my place in his life and in his heart.

I just couldn't sit back and watch her continue to disrespect me. Her time with him had expired on account of her disloyalty. If she failed to understand his cold shoulder, perhaps she would get it after I confronted her and told her to back off.

"I'll be back." I slid out of the booth, anxious to

join the heated conversation they were having on the other side of the restaurant.

"Mona... don't..." Monika reached for me, but I was too quick. I moved so fast that I glided across the expansive space in no time.

I hoped like hell they didn't follow me. An entourage was the last thing I needed. I could handle Veronica alone.

"Shit," Grayson mumbled when I approached them.

"Hello, handsome." I cuddled next to Donovan's side. Everyone around us vanished when he leaned down to kiss my cheek.

"What's up, beautiful?" He smiled. The tension that stressed his face when I was across the room diminished. It was the green light I needed to officially step in.

"What's going on?" I pulled my eyes from his to avoid getting lost in them.

Veronica's straight face disturbed me. She was no longer blushing in his face. My presence had shut it down.

"Nothing much. Veronica and her sister were just leaving." Donovan nodded toward the door, motioning for them to go.

"Let's just go," her sister whispered in her ear. I

sneered before I could control it. I couldn't stand a person who didn't know how to whisper properly. It was a pet peeve of mine. Or maybe everything was just irritating me at the moment.

I wasn't sure.

I only knew I wanted her to leave. She needed to bounce before I acted worse than my facial expressions were behaving.

"Something funny?" Veronica asked. She put her hand on her hip, poking it out as she side-eyed me.

"Yes." I stepped forward. Donovan grabbed me before I could reach her.

"Is she worth that?" He kissed my ear after he spoke in it.

The commotion mixed with the crowds of patrons surrounding us were draining enough. Then, he just had to whisper in my ear, setting my body ablaze from his authority over me.

"I'll see them out." Grayson stepped in.

"We don't need anyone to see us out," Veronica snarled, making a scene on her way to the door. Responding was out of the question. Dragging her out by her hair like I envisioned on the walk over was voided, too.

Donovan whisked me to the back, locking me

inside of his office. He blocked the door and stared at me as I paced back and forth in front of his desk.

"Is this going to be a frequent thing?" I looked him up and down. "If you think I'm going to put up with that shit." I laughed to myself. "You're wrong."

I wasn't mad at Donovan, but I was mad.

Just mad.

"Mona." He sighed.

"Is there something I don't know? Be real with me. Is there? I trust you, Donovan. I swear I do. But I need to know if that bitch is truly off her rocker, or if you're giving her some type of hope. Any indication that—"

"Mona." He pushed away from the door and inched toward me.

"If it's the latter, you can have that crazy bitch."

"It couldn't possibly be the latter. That shit doesn't even sound right."

"Then call her in here and I'll beat her ass right now."

Donovan chuckled as he lifted me off my feet. Sitting me on the edge of his desk, he parted my legs to stand between them.

"Why would I let you get your hands dirty like that?" He held my hand to his chest after I attempted pushing him back. "I'm sorry." He rubbed the back of his hand along the side of my cheek. "It won't happen again. I'll handle it."

"How? I watch enough Lifetime Movie Network movies to know she won't stop. Have you seen the movie *Obsessed*? We have to kill her."

Donovan's eyes widened. "She isn't the only crazy one among us, huh?"

"You damn right." I rolled my eyes and folded my arms across my chest.

A soft kiss on my neck calmed me down. He knew my spots. All of them. Donovan's touch never missed its mark.

"I'm sorry, Mona. Your peacefulness is one of the reasons I fell in love with you. I know this shit bothers you. I'm not sure what it will take to get her to stop, but I'll find a way. I'll do whatever it takes. In the meantime, you know my heart is yours, right?"

"Yeah." I rolled my eyes again. This time, a smile was attached to the end of my performance. I failed to play hard to get with him. "I know," I said.

"The fired-up Mona is sexy as fuck, though." He bit his bottom lip and tugged at my jeans.

"Donovan." I squealed. "My sisters are waiting for me."

"It's all good. I just need a quickie."

I tried swatting his hand away, but his strength always overpowered mine. Especially when he craved me.

"You don't understand the concept of a quick-ie," I reminded him.

"They can wait," he said. "It's not like they're paying for their meals anyway."

"I have to be back at work in two hours."

"Fuck that job. You don't have to work if you don't want to. I'll take care of you."

A passionate kiss ceased my response. His tongue parted my lips, commencing a tongue war that had me moaning in his mouth.

"Donovan. Wait." I panted between our sloppy kisses. He was more aggressive than usual. It excited me yet frightened me at the same time.

"For what?" he asked. Nonetheless, he paused for a moment. My needs and wants were always first in line to his. I never imagined loving a man as selfless as him.

Standing from his desk, I dropped to my knees and cupped his balls through his black slacks. His hard dick was suffocating. It ached to be released. Donovan looked down at me; his honey brown eyes gazed into mine as I unbuckled his belt.

Pulling his slacks to his ankles, I yanked at his briefs.

My mouth watered as I admired his thick shaft. I wasted no time swirling my tongue around the head of it. Precum greeted me with a confession that he couldn't resist me.

He never could.

After tucking stray strands of my hair behind my ears, I wrapped my arms around his waist. I looked up at him with glossy eyes, fighting through the urge to gag while he fucked my mouth.

The vibration of my moan made him grab both sides of my head. He was gentle as he pumped in and out of my mouth. And gentle as he cursed under his breath, pissed off at his buckling knees.

Unable to take anymore, he stepped back and shook his head. I was proud of his resistance. And I was anxious to feel him inside of me like I knew he desperately wanted to be. With his index finger at the tip of my chin, he summoned me to stand.

"Tell me," he said, sucking my bottom lip in his mouth. Donovan backed me into his desk and peeled my skin-tight jeans down my thighs inch by inch.

"Fuck me, Donovan."

I giggled, amused when he bent me over his

desk and rubbed his large hands over my ass like it was a crystal ball. Then, I gasped when I felt his dick at my entrance. Donovan moved the string of my thong aside. I winced at the pressure and closed my eyes as I prepared for him to fill me up.

"Relax," he whispered in my ear, then leaned into me to kiss my cheek. "And take this dick," he demanded, wrapping his hand around my neck.

For him, I was happy to oblige.

For Donovan Powell, I accepted every inch like a good girl.

Chapter 6

DONOVAN

I parked alongside the curb in front of my childhood home.

My father was caught up in the weeds he was snatching from my mother's garden. I snuck up on him and chuckled at the scowl on his face.

"Your wife got you out here baking in the sun, huh? She tricked you into taking care of her garden. You're whipped."

"You better watch your mouth when you're talking to me, boy." He stood up from the soil and clapped his hands clean. His scowl from the heat slowly relaxed into a smile.

Looking at my father was like looking into a mirror. My own reflection stared back at me. The gray in his beard was the only indication that we weren't twins. Despite him being twenty years older than me, our features mirrored one another. The man hardly aged and I appreciated that. I looked forward to old age because of it.

"How are you doing, Son?" He grabbed me into his arms and patted my back.

"I'm good, Pops. I brought y'all some food from the Smokehouse." I offered him the tall, brown bags in my hand. "Figured Mom wasn't up for cooking tonight."

"You figured right." He latched onto the straw handles on the paper bags. "And since we're on the subject of being whipped—"

"Aw, c'mon, Dad." I waved him off and headed for the front door.

He was on my trail, clowning me with no remorse.

"We hardly see you. Don't tell me she only releases you to let you go to work these days."

I could only chuckle. Truth is, I only left Mona's side when I had to work. If it were up to me, she wouldn't work. I would convince her to tag along with me every hour of the day.

Yeah. I was whipped.

We found my mom in the kitchen, which was nothing out of the ordinary. She always read articles on her tablet or played crossword puzzles while sitting at the center island. She gossiped on the phone in the kitchen and spied on the neighbors from the window. The kitchen had been her haven since I was a child. Overtime, it became my haven, too. My love for cooking kept me there.

"I'll call you back, Mary. Jr is here." My mom jumped down carefully from her high-stool. She rounded the wide, circular island to hug me, then squealed over me with the phone to her ear. "Yes, I'll tell him you said hello. Talk to you later," she said, disconnecting their call.

"How are you, baby?" Though I towered over her five-foot-even height, I knew to lean down whenever she greeted me. She rubbed my cheek every time she asked about my well-being. She used to tell me her instincts kicked in quicker when she was hands on with me.

"I'm good, Mom. Just stopped by to drop off some food for you and Dad to try. Grayson put a note on the new entrees we've added to the menu."

"God bless you, Son. Your father has been trying to get me to cook all week." She looked back at him and laughed. My father, who was a big fan of my mother's home cooked meals, didn't find anything amusing.

"How is Mona doing?" She looped her arm in mine and guided me to the nearest stool.

"She's good," I assured her. "I can't stay long, Mom."

"And why not? You're always in a rush to leave when you visit us. Stay a while. Help your father with the garden," she said.

My father washed his hands, then went into the refrigerator for a bottle of water. He laughed on his way back to the front door.

"All right, Mom." I gave in to her golden-brown eyes.

It made her happy to watch us together from the kitchen window. Denying her that luxury was impossible. We'd never said *no* to Kate Powell before, and we wouldn't start now. Her loving features wouldn't allow it. Her glowing brown skin and nurturing voice did the trick.

"That's one bossy woman," I said.

Kneeling next to my father, I tugged at the unruly weeds surrounding my mom's tulips.

"That's what I love about her," he said. "What's on your mind, Don?"

"What do you mean?"

Something's bothering you."

"What makes you think that?" I asked. I

glanced back and forth from him and the garden of tulips and orchids. They were my mother's favorite flowers.

"You're my son," was all he said.

"Pops." I sighed. "Veronica's back."

"Is that right?" He laughed. "And you're shocked about that?"

"You're not? She played me. She made her choice."

"She realizes she made the wrong choice."

"Yeah, but it's too late for that. I'm happy with Mona and she's trying to mess that up for me. Louisville isn't big enough for the both of us anymore. Today was the second day she popped up. Mona was around both times. What am I supposed to do?"

"Nothing."

"*Nothing?*" I scoffed.

"You do nothing, Jr," he said. "You reassure Mona, of course. You love her, so you make that clear to her. But you do nothing about Veronica. That'll get through to her quicker than you trying to reason with her. Love your woman out loud and do nothing about the mess that tries to come in between that, Son. Be still."

"I sure hope that'll work."

"Trust me," he concluded. "It works."

"Hold your head up, Son," he stated firmly. "What have me and your mother always taught you about confusion?" He looked into my eyes.

After motioning me to stand tall with him, he stood directly in front of me. By the time I was seventeen, I'd caught up to his height of six-five, making us even from there.

"*For God is not the author of confusion,*" I began. "One Corinthians, fourteen-thirty-three."

"That's right. Resist the devil and he will flee from you," he finished. "That means, ignore the bull—"

"Dad." I cut him off and chuckled. "I feel you. I understand."

"All right then," he said. "Thought I was gon' have to speak your language for a minute," he quipped, pulling me into a firm hold. "What's for you is for you, Jr. The past can't stop that."

"Thank you, Pops. I appreciate you, old man." I patted his stomach that seemed to poke out more and more these days.

"Chill on my pot of gold." He swatted my hand away before kneeling down to pull weeds again.

The wave of relief that overcame me was soothing. And just like that, I had a masterplan in place to handle Veronica… by not handling her at all.

———

Too much wasn't enough.

Nah.

I wanted Mona at all times—during all hours of the day.

After leaving my parent's house, I headed straight to my loft. Her work hours lasted two hours longer than mine. Speeding home to prepare for her arrival made me happy. I was overly content with that shit.

I was proud to run her a warm bath every night, filled with her favorite bubble bath and surrounded by her favorite vanilla Yankee candles.

I knew I was her man. No denying that. I felt like the man when I took care of her. Like the world was beneath me and I towered over it. She made me feel in control of the world.

When her small gap was on full display, there was no better feeling than the glee that came from witnessing that. Mona's aura uplifted me and made me feel on top of the world. She was invincible and untouchable.

The digital dashboard in my car lit up, displaying Mona's name and the water drop emoji she'd stored next to her name long ago. I smirked every time I saw it. The visual representation had nothing on her, but I appreciated the reminder. My head between her thighs was my favorite place to be whenever her juices flowed.

I pressed a button on my wheel to connect us. "Talk to me, beautiful," I answered, anxious to hear the angelic voice I loved.

"Hi daddy," she cooed into the phone. Her sultry voice was activated and ready to seduce me.

That only meant one thing.

"Go ahead and tell me what you want, Princess. It's yours."

Mona giggled. "I'm going to be a little late making it home," she said.

For a moment, I was stuck.

Dazed.

"Run that by me again," I said.

I needed to hear it again. Had to hear it again.

"I know, I know. I miss you too, but Molli has summoned me to her house. She said she needs to tell me something face to face. Like we didn't just have lunch together earlier," she rambled. "Maybe she couldn't tell me whatever it is in front of Monika."

"Aye, don't trip, baby. Just make it to me when you can. I just wanted you to repeat the *home* part. I like the sound of that."

"Well, it does feel like home when I'm there. Whether you're there with me or not, I feel protected in your space."

"How long have you felt like that?" I asked. My pride was through the roof. Putting it aside for her was easy, but she definitely added onto it. Mona boosted my ego by simply looking at me.

"For a while," she whispered. "Since the first night I slept over with you."

"Oh?"

"Mhm. The night you kissed every inch of my body. You held me until I fell asleep, and then you whispered in my ear when you thought I was. You promised to protect me. You swore to never break my heart, and you told me you love me. You told me you loved me before officially telling me you were *in* love with me."

I was silent, taken aback and *in* love. In love with a flawed woman who was flawless to me. Her chocolate skin and beautiful brown eyes made me putty in her hands.

"I love you, Donovan. So much." She snapped me out of the trance I was under, saving me before I got further lost in my thoughts while on the road.

"I love you too, beautiful. See you soon."

Before we disconnected our call, she made me blow kisses over the phone. Mona was the only women who could get me to do some corny shit like that. Not even a second after we disconnected our call, I missed her. I missed her like I hadn't seen her all day.

It'd been an insightful year knowing her. She introduced me to a peace I'd never known. I let the hurt go and welcomed serenity into my heart. Then, six months into knowing her, I asked her to be mine.

To belong to me.

To believe in me and not judge how quickly I'd fallen in love with her.

Mona Hill was the woman for me.

Chapter 7

MONA

I entered Molli's house with the spare key she gave me on the day she purchased the two-story home. Becoming a home owner was one of her great accomplishments. Some days, she was sad she didn't have a family of her own to share it with. However, every day, she was content with being a best-selling author who could afford the luxurious lifestyle she created for herself.

Molli specialized in thriller plots that blew minds. Readers had no idea who she truly was or how she looked. For three years, she'd been signed to one of the biggest publishing companies in the country. Each novel she released hit number one in her category, and her supporters would never personally know the brilliant, bad-mouth, goofy girl behind the pen.

Molli preferred it that way.

She wanted to do what she loved without the extra pressure to show up and defend it. It took her a year to tell our parents she was an author. Her *M. Hill* pen name blew up unexpectedly, and it was only a matter of time before our parents noticed the abundance of money she frequently spent on them.

"I'm in the living room, Mona," she shouted from afar. She'd been settled in her home for over eight months, but there was still an echo in it. Our voices boomed and bounced off the tall, teal walls.

Molli didn't know how she wanted her home decorated, so she'd only purchased the minimum— a love seat, a glass table, coasters for our wine glasses, and a large wooden bookshelf. Of course, there was a high, queen-sized bed in her bedroom, but that was where the details of her home ended.

Monika and I shared an ongoing joke with each other that Molli's home was her own personal insane asylum. It was empty, cold and filled with voices of the crazy characters' she created and wrote about.

"Girl, what is going on?" I stood in front of the couch, staring at her top her wine glass.

"Want some?" She poured a small taste in an empty glass next to hers. She'd always been stingy with her Dom Perignon.

"Sure." I sat next to her on the purple, suede loveseat, anxiously awaiting whatever came next. "Molli." I huffed. "C'mon now."

"Fine. I'm just going to come out and tell you. May as well, huh? It is what it is."

"Get it off your chest then." I laughed at her theatrics.

Fucking middle child syndrome!

"I'm a whore," she said, shaking her head. "I skipped out on having a hoe phase in my twenties. It's happening now. At thirty."

"You're going to have to fill my glass to the rim if this is an intervention," I quipped and reached for the bottle to top my glass. "You became a whore overnight? Am I missing something?"

My sisters and I shared everything with each other. It's how we were raised. Our parents taught us to depend on each other. To be loyal and always take care of one another. Either Molli had been keeping secrets from the squad or she'd become a *whore* overnight... or, maybe even after our lunch outing together.

"You had a one-night stand or something?" I slanted my eyes at her.

"Grayson." She closed her eyes and exhaled deeply.

"Excuse me? *Grayson* who? I know we aren't talking about Grayson *Steel*, Donovan's business partner. I just know it can't be—"

"That's him," she confirmed.

"You had sex with Grayson? Even after my warning? So, you're living life on the edge like the women in your novels now?"

"Pipe down please." She stood from the couch and paced in front of me.

"Molli, you're flaring my damn anxiety."

"We kissed okay! A lot. And for a long time. All I did was introduce myself to him. I left the booth to look for you. To make sure you were okay. Next thing I know, I'm in his office swapping spit with a fucking stranger. A fine ass stranger, might I add."

"Swapping spit?" I burst out laughing. "Yup." I nodded to confirm her previous claim. "A whore. That's who you are!"

"I hate your guts." She rolled her eyes. "Don't joke right now, Mona. This really happened."

"Fine. "I'm sorry. Tell me what happened next."

"I ran out of his office. He tried to stop me, but

my legs wouldn't stop moving. I was out of there and back at our booth like nothing happened."

"That's it?" My eyes widened.

"Molli nodded vigorously. "I kept my head down for the rest of the time we were there, then I rushed out of the restaurant after we were done eating."

"Come to think of it, you were the first one out of the door," I whispered to myself, thinking back on the eventful day.

"Now I can't stop thinking about him. I close my eyes and relive our kiss. I touch my lips and remember his being there. I feel connected to him. I want to kiss him again, Mona."

"I warned you about him."

"Don't start."

"I warned you about him and you went and kissed him, linking yourself to him."

"Mona, it just happened! Like it was bound to happen. Like it was destined or something."

"Your track record," I mentioned. I didn't judge my sisters. We didn't judge each other. But Molli's track record of men was horrendous. Her attraction to bad boys and assholes was beyond me. "You certainly have a type."

"Molli plopped down next to me and huffed.

She mumbled under her breath, probably cursing me out and regretting her decision to tell me about her *life-changing* kiss with Grayson.

"Just forget I told you anything," she said.

"Molli, don't make this personal. I'm just—"

"Before you *finally* got it right with Donovan, your track record was shitty, too. Comical even," she reminded me. And I hated her for it, but I understand why she needed to remind me.

"You're right." I chugged the remnants of my wine to shake my bad nerves. Invading her space, I snuggled closer to her and rested my head on her shoulder. "I'm sorry. I didn't mean to throw anything in your face or rehash the past. That's the last thing I want to do. You deserve the best, Molli. I don't care how cliché it sounds. Facts are facts," I said.

"I know you mean well, sis." She rubbed my head and sighed.

"…are facts," I added to my previous sentiment.

"Shut up." She laughed.

"Do you want me to get his number for you?" I asked, hopeful she would deny it, but still willing to get it for her if she accepted the bait.

"God, no. I'm in book mode starting Monday morning. I have a release date coming up really soon. The last thing I need is a distraction that fine. A distraction who smells that good. A distraction with a dick print that—"

"My goodness, Molli," I cut her off. "Sounds like you're already distracted to me."

"For your information, I'm inspired," she countered. "And distracted." She whined.

"You have the weekend to get him out of your system."

"I'm never eating at your boyfriend's restaurant again. I'll order from Uber Eats and deal with their scamming ass taxes, fees, and ghetto drivers before I do."

"Are you going to tell Monika about this?" I asked.

"Not for a long time." Molli scoffed. "I'll tell her when I'm over it. I'm not in the mood to be judged by a happily married woman who's only ever been in love with one man."

"See! You see why I tell her things late? Everyone isn't able to live the good life like her. She doesn't understand our struggle."

"*Our*? The struggle is over for you. I'm in this alone now," she whispered, resting her head on top of mine.

"You won't be for long," I assured her. "You're

an amazing daughter, sister, friend and author. You're so many amazing things, Molli. True love will find you just like success did. It's been written in the stars already, and you will get all the good your heart deserves. Have faith in that."

"I love you, sis. Thank you for coming over."

"Anytime," I promised.

"The struggle is over for you," echoed in my head.

I prayed she was right. I hoped like hell that I finally got it right. Lord knows Donovan felt magically correct to me.

My heart praised him.

My body craved him.

Being in love with him was an understatement.

But what else could I say?

How else could I put it?

I wouldn't change a thing about Donovan, not even the things I could change. He was perfect for me.

The struggle is over for you.

I closed my eyes and smiled. If it took enduring drama and heartache to reach this point, my regrets were officially dismissed. I would no longer regret a thing because he was worth the hassle. Donovan's love was the light at the end of a dark tunnel.

The struggle was over.

———

HE WAS ASLEEP WHEN I GOT IN. IT WAS THE FIRST time I had to utilize the key he'd given me. His bedroom smelled just like his Shea Butter Old Spice body wash. Its strong and masculine smell filled the room. I remembered the first night it crawled up my nostrils and suffocated me. However, I didn't remember if I initially hated it. I only knew I loved it now. I inhaled it on his smooth, brown skin every night before bed.

The lamp next to his side of the bed was on, and the comic section of the newspaper laid across his bare stomach, right above the light blue sheet that covered the rest of his body. I pulled out my phone to snap a photo of him. I needed proof that he was a fifty-year-old man in a twenty-eight-year-old muscular body. I teased him often about it, and he despised when I called him my sugar daddy.

Careful not to wake him, I glided around the room light as a feather. I unclothed to take a shower and closed the door softly behind me, then aired a silent prayer to not wake him. Besides my father, Donovan was the hardest working man I'd ever known.

After a long day at work, I loved rubbing

through his short-cut until he drifted off to sleep. If he couldn't get peace from anywhere else, he would always find it in me. Hard-working men of his stature deserved that.

I showered quickly to make it back to him. To rush back to bed and cuddle next to him. Thankfully, he was still there when I got out the shower and threw on one of his shirts. His beard glistened from the Aloe Vera beard conditioner he used every morning and night. He lied on his back, completely still as his chest occasionally moved up and down.

After removing the newspaper from his chest, I cut off the lamp on his marble nightstand. Then, I circled around the bed to crawl in on my side. Once my head connected with his chest, life was complete.

What more could I ask for?

"Hey, beautiful." He groaned and pulled me closer to his side. Any closer and I would've been on top of him.

"Hi, baby. Sorry to wake you."

"Don't be. Tell me about your day," he said. It never failed. He always asked about my day. Usually, I gave him an earful. I wouldn't hesitate to fill him in on my coworkers, clients, sisters and whatever else took place during the day.

Tonight, was different.

I wanted to be held. I only wanted to bask in his ambience until I fell asleep and woke up next to him in the morning.

"Kiss me," I whispered and met his soft lips halfway.

I moaned as our tongues danced together. I had to force myself to pull back before it got too deep, and I hated that I was too tired to have my world rocked by him.

"I'll tell you over breakfast," I said.

"Deal."

Ending the night in his arms was the best part of my day.

Chapter 8

DONOVAN

If looks could kill, Mona would've gotten me out of here. Her brown eyes shot daggers through me and her sudden silence worried me.

"You think I'm dumb, don't you? You already knew, and you're sitting up here listening to me, pretending you didn't know."

"Mona—"

"What did Grayson say about Molli?" Leaning against the countertop, she tossed a grape in her mouth. Feeding them to me was no more. We were officially beefin' at ten in the morning.

"He's been wanting to talk to her since the first time y'all visited the Smokehouse."

"Is that what he said?"

"Mona, that's what I know. He was supposed to make the same move I did with you. He dropped the ball. He was too scared to speak to her that day."

"That man isn't scared of anything."

I chuckled. "You know what I mean." Pulling her closer to me, I roamed underneath her shirt. Her body was warm, soft and silk in my hands. "What's your issue with my brother, woman?"

"I don't have an issue with him." She whimpered from my touch. "He's a player and I don't want my sister to get hurt."

"He's a single man," I said. The frown on her face told me she didn't agree with me defending his promiscuous ways. "Men change for the woman they want to be with. We don't have to be asked, warned, threatened or bribed. It happens naturally for the woman we know we need. Maybe Grayson hasn't met that woman yet."

"You're saying Molli could be that woman for him?"

I shrugged and leaned down to kiss her cheek. "Could be."

She hissed when I sat her on top of the cold countertop. Mona went back to feeding me grapes while playing in my beard. Her frown transformed into the beautiful smile I loved.

"Did you change for me?"

"I didn't have to. I changed for myself a long time ago. I was ready for a woman like you."

"A woman like me?"

I hit her with a simple nod. It was all I was willing to give at the moment.

"You've been mean to me all morning because my brother kissed your sister. I'm not up for gassin' you up right now."

"Aww. Don't be like that. I'm running on E. You haven't gassed me up in a while."

"Bullshit." I squeezed her thighs. "Your tank runneth over." I laughed at her attempt to butter me up. Mona cupped the side of my face and gazed into my eyes. She drew me forward, meeting me halfway to crash her lips into mine.

"You were saying?" She broke our kiss and bat her lashes.

"I was ready for a woman as intelligent as you," I started. I smoothed my hand over her wild hair and smiled. Her beautiful ass had me wrapped around her finger.

"Mhm." She blushed. "Continue."

"A woman as kind. Nurturing. Beautiful inside and out—"

"Sounds about right."

"A woman with her own. One who doesn't need me for shit but appreciates everything I bring to the table anyway. You let me be your man. You let me front the bill and take care of you to hold onto that title. I appreciate that."

She nestled her head against my neck. "I'm pretty full now. Tell me more later?"

"Anytime." I kissed her forehead. "Are you up for spending your Saturday with your man?"

"Yes, please. Can we go see the new Toy Story movie?"

"Yeah, I'll take your grown ass to see Toy Story."

"Thank you, handsome." She wrapped her arms around my neck.

"You know I got you."

"Thank you for everything, Donovan. You make me feel safe and secure in our relationship. It calms me down. It soothes my soul. I know it's love."

"It's been a pleasure loving you, Mona."

———

I was half an hour late to poker night with the boys. To be real, I'd forgotten all about it.

Once a week, I met up with Grayson and a couple of our friends to catch up, talk shit and take each other's money. We drank beer, filled each other in on whatever was new, and hung out for a few hours. We usually met up at Grayson's condo and left without cleaning up after ourselves. He never complained.

"This guy." One of our homeboys, James, answered the door laughing. After bumping fists with him, I brushed past him.

"Loverboy finally made it," Grayson said. James and Leland joined in on the fun. They clowned me right along with him.

"Aye, man. Fuck all y'all." I waved them off and made a beeline to the cooler next to the poker set-up for a beer.

"Mona has our mans' wide open," Grayson persisted.

"You might want to chill on me," I threatened with a sly smile. I chuckled when his laughter stopped. He glared at me and mouthed for me not to utter a word of his business. The kiss he shared with Mona's sister had fucked his head up.

I couldn't blame him. Them Hill sisters were something else.

"Y'all ready to start the game or what?" I took my position, ready to beat their ass in the game and take their money like I frequently did. I didn't always win, but my winning streaks were ahead of theirs.

"Man, where you been?" Leland sat across from me. "Got the nerve to be late and then come in here bossing us around."

"My fault. Mona wanted to see a movie."

"Oh word? What y'all see?" James asked.

"Toy Story," I tried to mumble, but Leland caught on right away.

"Don't be ashamed, man," he said. "My girl talked me into that shit, too. Had me in there holding her while she cried and shit." He shook his head.

"Your girl and mine would get alone well then," I said. "Mona cried, too."

"Yup. We gotta link 'em one day," Leland said. Though I nodded, I chuckled internally.

How could I tell him my girl wasn't friendly?

Respectful, yes. Kind even. But if it wasn't her sisters, Molli and Monika, she was good on hanging out with other women. Her inner circle was set.

I appreciated that about her. Access to Mona didn't come easy. She was a rare experience, meant to be treasured. Not everyone could handle her or be favored enough to behold her.

"I'll see what I can do," I said. I pulled a few bills from my pocket and slapped them on the table. "Y'all ready to put your money where your mouth is?"

The shit talking had commenced on my end.

Chapter 9

MONA

I loved it when we missed each other. Granted, we always did. The feeling was inevitable the second we parted ways. But, I lavished in the way he embraced me and kissed all over my face after a long day of missing me. Because of that, I encouraged him to attend his regularly scheduled poker night with his friends.

Not to mention, I needed to check on my condo, feed my goldfish, Piper and Taystee, if they were still alive, and catch up on financial reports for a new client.

My love life was thriving and my heart was proud of it. But I had to admit, it was my greatest distraction. If I could make a living lying under

Donovan every hour of the day, I wouldn't have hesitated to jump on the opportunity.

Inside of my condo, I checked every room while smiling at the beauty and stillness of it all. I'd missed my bright space. The purple tint from the lavender curtains in each room warmed me up inside. I'd been meaning to suggest we spend more time at my place, but I failed to mention it. Once I made it into Donovan's arms, it always slipped my mind.

Excited to see my goldfish were still alive, well and swimming around in their small tank that sat on top of the glass table beside the sofa, I rushed over to feed them. I watched them make it to the top in record time where the food pebbles floated. They nipped at the pieces until they were full and satisfied.

Procrastination was coming on full force. As I stood in the middle of my living room, my wide eyes roamed every inch of it like it was the first time I'd ever witnessed it. I dragged myself to my home office and locked myself inside of the compact room. Distractions were little to none in there.

The room was simple. It was nearly empty and the white walls made it dull and boring. A large wooden desk with a black desk chair pushed in behind it occupied the room, along with the MacBook desktop that sat on top of it.

I plopped down onto the chair and twirled around in it. My workload was suffocating me, and it was all my fault. The longer I put things off, the more it became overbearing and a nuisance for me.

I made good money to organize my client's finances and income-based projects and I loved what I did. Despite how tedious it was, it remained a passion of mine and a task I was undeniably good at.

A grocery list that I'd never gotten to was stuck to my desktop screen. Tiny words were written on an orange sticky note. Butter Pecan ice cream was at the top of the list. Amongst everything else, that item stuck out to me the most.

Just that quick, I convinced myself I needed to make a store run. The Target two blocks over from my condo was calling my name.

The angel on my left shoulder was sighing and performing an epic facepalm. On the opposite shoulder, the procrastination devil was ready for me to explore the wondrous aisles of Target.

The possibilities would be endless once I walked through the sliding doors of my favorite place.

In under ten minutes, I was at Target, parked

and power-walking to the entrance as if I was in a rush to get in and out. It never worked out like that., anyway.

After sanitizing the handle of a cart with a Purell wipe, I pushed forward and headed straight for the unhealthy snacks I didn't need. They accompanied me best while I worked.

Suddenly, the wind was knocked out of me at the sight of her on the chip aisle.

Her.

Why did I have to run into her... alone?

My blood boiled as my body underwent changes I'd never experienced.

I couldn't breathe. That's what it felt like. Yet, I exhaled so deeply that she had no choice but to look back and notice me. When Veronica turned back, she examined me. Her flats were planted where she stood. She parted her lips to speak, but nothing came out.

Space and opportunity! Damn. The last time I saw her, I prayed for that.

Space and opportunity.

Veronica looked more pathetic than she did the previous time I saw her. I didn't understand why, but I suddenly felt sorry for her. Then, I remembered the disrespect and the courage she'd been acting on in a sad attempt to win Donovan back.

That did it.

The memories evoked my disgust with her all over again. My irritation with her was brought back to life and I scoffed at the sight of her before I knew it.

"Do you have something to say to me?" she asked while inching toward to me.

"I'm not much of a talker," I said. My heart raced as I fixed my hair in a bun on top of my head. Veronica had nerve.

The audacity!

Courage.

Boldness.

She had many commendable traits that would get her popped in this moment. Beyond anything else, she was disrespectful. I couldn't get over that main factor about her.

She stopped in her tracks and a staring contest commenced while neither of us blinked. I waited on her to move even closer to me. All I needed was an excuse.

A justifiable reason to take it there!

Failing to give me that, she turned her back to me. "I'm not doing this with you," she called behind her shoulder. "At the end of the day, Donovan will decide. Our history together can't be tossed out or forgotten. I'm sorry if it offends you."

"You're crazier than I thought." I laughed to restrain myself from shaking some common sense into her.

"Excuse me?" She snapped her neck in my direction. Her hair moved with her, bouncing over her shoulders with each move she made.

"The history you speak of has been acknowledged. Every part of it, whether good or bad, has been discussed, picked apart and considered. He's expressed the good in you, but he's also noted the bad, which is most of what you've shown him." My eyes were set on hers. I felt nothing as hers watered.

"Donovan has chosen. At the end of the day, it's me. Top of the morning, it's me. Middle of the evening..." I smiled just thinking about him. "Well, you get it. He's happy. With me. He made his decision a long time ago, crazy ass girl," I said, and she stormed away. I only blinked once before she rounded the corner and disappeared before my eyes.

"Crazy ass girl," I mumbled to myself, then turned faced the shelves. The decision between choosing between Spicy Nacho Doritos or Pretzels with no salt had taken over my mind.

Just that fast, Veronica was out of sight and off my mind.

My body was still on an agitated high. Though my sandals were planted where I stood, my legs shook and my knees buckled. They threatened to take me down unless I followed her and said more of what I'd been wanting to say to her. My restraint shocked me when I didn't.

Molli and Monika would've been proud of me for holding back. I claimed I wasn't much of a talker, but I for damn sure had more to say to Veronica. I had more to point out and prove to her.

The man she wanted went out of his way every day to cater to me. If Veronica needed proof of who Donovan's heart craved and cried out for, she was looking at her. I was his heart in human form.

Once I reminded myself of the facts, my agitation settled down. I realized I had Donovan. I had the man she almost ruined.

The brick atmosphere in Target usually bothered me. This visit was different, though. My run-in with Veronica heated things up.

Then, there was Donovan.

One thought of him did it for me.

Veronica just couldn't compete where she didn't compare. If she would've paid attention to how he looked at me, she would've kept her distance after the first pop-up. If only she was aware of all the gentle and attentive ways he cared for me. She would've never showed face.

Suddenly, I was in an eager mood to shop and sight see the aisles of Target like it was a beautiful, foreign country instead of an expansive shopping center.

It felt good to be confident within Donovan's love, and to be certain of his love for me even while I was under his spell. Our love wasn't pseudo. Our connection wasn't a façade.

At the end of the day, he had chosen me. Top of the morning, he awakened just to please me. Middle of the evening, I remained the apple of his eye.

Donovan was all about me.

"Crazy ass girl," I mumbled to myself.

Chapter 10
DONOVAN

I was always the last one to leave Grayson's crib when poker night concluded. All other times, it was unintentional. Tonight, was different. I needed to see what was up with him.

He'd been playing the game with us, but his focus was elsewhere. We clowned his sucker tactics all night and he hardly retaliated. Something was going on in his head, or someone was taking over his mind. I had a strong feeling it was the latter.

"Aye man—"

"I don't know what's wrong with me, Don," he cut me off. "This isn't me! I don't trip over women." He scoffed. "I can't live without them, that's for sure." He chuckled to himself. "But I don't trip over them. What the fuck them Hill sisters be doing to men? Voodoo or something?"

"Something," I said and grabbed a bottle of water from the fridge.

"I held that crease between her lil stomach and thighs when I kissed her, man. That's what fucked me up."

"G." I dropped my head, trying my hardest not to laugh in his face. He had it bad already. And I knew exactly how he felt.

"Oh, you think it's a game?"

"No. I know it's not. This is nothing. The motions get worse."

"I'm not looking forward to that."

"Me either. You trippin', G. I never thought I would see the day."

"I need her number," he said. The look in his eyes was inexplainable. Desperation was how I interpreted it. Whether it was a call, text, or being near her again, he needed that. And man had I been there before!

"You want me to take care of that for you?"

Grayson shook his head and rubbed over his beard in deep thought. "She has to give it to me on her own."

"I'm glad you feel the way because I would've

had to go through my shorty's phone for you. Molli told her what happened and…" My laughter cut me short. Grayson's thoughtful expression transformed into a smile. He leaned against the counter, cheesing hard with slanted eyes.

"She already choppin' it up about me, huh?"

"Yeah, man. And I'm already getting threatened by Mona over you. If you on some bullshit, leave Molli alone. I will never hear the last of it."

"Do I act like this when I'm on some bullshit, D? Have you ever seen me act like this?" G was turning defensive on me. His smile faded instantly. "Look. I don't know what I'm on, but I know it ain't bullshit."

"All right, G." I pulled him into a brotherly hug before I bounced. "I hear you. I got you."

"Bet." He walked me to the door. "You can find me at the Smokehouse tomorrow if you need me. I'm behind on a few reports."

"I damn sure won't come looking for you there," I said.

Grayson would live in the Smokehouse if he could. Sunday's were the only day the restaurant was closed, and he still showed up to work bright and early. I appreciated having a business partner as dedicated as him, but Sunday was the one day I refused to even drive by the restaurant, let alone sit inside and take care of paperwork all day.

"I'm already knowing," he quipped. "Drive safe, brother. Shoot me a quick text when you make it home."

"I got you."

"And tell Mona to mind her business for me."

"I'll tell her in spirit," I said.

———

"Did you think I wouldn't come looking for you?" I cupped her cheek when she opened her door. Too many hours without touching her was turning me into a mad man. The warmth of her cheek replenished my soul.

"I knew you would." She held my hand to her face. "Come in," she whispered and tugged on my arm. "Please."

I chuckled at her sweet innocence. As if she ever had to beg me to do anything.

"Did you win?" she asked excitedly after we plopped down onto the love seat.

"I don't want to talk about it."

"Aww, baby."

Mona straddled my lap and wrapped her arms

around my neck. She didn't believe in being dressed while she was inside. Only an oversized T-shirt was drenched over her stunning, thick body—one of my many T-shirts that she jacked from my closet.

"It's all good."

"No, it's not." She nestled her head against my neck and inhaled me. "You're a sore loser."

"Word?"

"I hate to break it to you."

"You didn't have to." I tickled her sides, drawing out the pitchy giggles that I loved.

"I hate how much I miss you when we're apart. Is it even normal to miss you like that?" she asked.

"I've never cared much for normal." Mona lifted her head to gaze into my eyes.

A wide smile formed on her face. A contagious smile that I matched within seconds of witnessing it.

"Good, because we're far from normal. Our love is over the top. Our intimacy, on all levels, is beyond anything I've ever experienced or imagined."

"Six months together," I said.

"One year knowing each other," she whispered against my lips, eyeing my beard with a seductive smile.

I kissed her bottom lip. "Thank God you're here."

"Ditto." Exhaling deeply, she laid her head on my chest.

"I need to show you something."

I prided myself on always being honest with her. Mona would always hear it from me before anyone else had a chance to relay the message.

"Show me then," she said.

Her sweet voice was already tempting enough. Mona's thin, black lace panties weren't making things easier for me. I was surprised she even had those on. The access to her treat was still easy, though, and my restraint was diminishing.

I moved her from my lap to sit her on the cushion beside me.

"Is it *that* serious?" she asked, and I held back from laughing. If she had it her way, she would remain on my lap at all times.

"It's nothing that'll break us because there isn't anything that can. I just... I feel affirmed with you, Mona. I feel good. I'm finally getting the love I deserve. You feel me?" She nodded slowly, a nervous smile curling her lips. "I need to return that feeling to you in every way. That includes being honest and reassuring you every step of the way."

"What is it?" Though her smile faded away, she was still soft—so damn soft and vulnerable with me. She trusted me with everything inside of her; that much was obvious at this point in our relationship.

"Veronica texted me." I dug into my pocket to hand her my phone. Inside my phone, she would find a long message from my ex. She'd poured her heart out via text message, ending it with a, *goodbye, until we meet again in another lifetime*, line at the end of it.

I was good on meeting again, in this lifetime or the next, but I appreciated her willingness to move on and leave me alone.

"Just tell me what the message says, Donovan." Mona denied the opportunity to unlock my phone and read the message for herself. Instead, she sat it on the coffee table in front of us and stared at me for answers.

"To summarize it, she said she will always love me but she's happy I'm happy with you. She promised to respect our relationship and keep her distance from here on out."

Mona burst into laughter.

"What's up with you?" I chuckled, reeling her onto my lap again. "What's funny?"

"She's funny. I saw her at the Target on West-brook earlier today. The one a couple blocks over."

"Mona." I brushed my hand down my face. "Do you need to turn yourself in to the police?"

"I didn't touch that girl, Donovan." She folded her arms across her chest. "And she didn't tempt me either. She's a smart girl. She knows how far to take it. I only talked to her."

"You talked?"

"Talked," she confirmed with her head held high.

"Should I be—"

"Don't worry about it." She kissed my cheek and then my lips.

The perfect distraction.

"Something I said must've hit home for her." She shrugged. "I'm glad she came to her senses."

"You're a bad woman." I slapped her ass, squeezing it firmly thereafter.

"And you're *my* man."

Underneath her, my dick was hard and aching to be released from my pants. Mona unbuckled my belt and snatched it from the loops. Tossing the belt aside, she dropped to her knees, released my dick, then kissed the head of it.

"Sometimes, all I can think about is sucking your dick."

I smiled and groaned when she slid half of my dick inside her mouth. Mona had a lot of good embedded in her, but deep down inside, she was as naughty as they come.

I held her head back by her hair to admire her gorgeous face. "It's going to be a long night for you," I warned—a warning she should've been used to by now.

A request to fuck her mouth emitted from her as a seductive, desperate plea. She knew I would give her whatever she wanted, and she would never have to ask for anything twice. I kept her hair wrapped around my fist, gradually sliding inside and out of her mouth.

Her beauty was a distraction. Choosing between owning my dominance or taking my time to admire her was a tough decision.

Mona swirled her tongue around my dick.

"Shit," I cursed through the pleasure. I tried to step back but failed to take control.

Mona held onto me. One of her soft hands gripped my thigh, holding me in place. The other hand on my ass, pushing me forward until my dick touched the back of her throat, making her gag.

After coming up for air, she still refused to quit. She kissed the head of my dick and cupped my balls, massaging them tenderly as she opened wide to accept me in her mouth again. I didn't want her on her knees anymore. Mona's body was a beautiful maze. A curvy, scrumptious maze that I loved to explore.

"Up." I released her hair, staring into her eyes until she stood and awaited further instruction from me.

Making love to her never left my mind. The visual remained there. Mona's dark skin amazed me every time I took it in.

"Sixty seconds," I moved her hair aside and spoke near her ear. My top lip grazed her diamond stud earring. "I want you naked and on all fours when I walk into your bedroom. You have sixty seconds."

Before she ran into her bedroom to prepare for me, she grabbed my dick and rose on her toes to kiss my lips.

"Sixty seconds, it is," she said.

Chapter 11

MONA

"**D**o you ever miss her?" I asked, lying on his chest. Donovan was half asleep, but I had to ask. The question had been on the tip of my tongue all night, taunting me relentlessly.

"Who?" his deep baritone mumbled. His hand that rested at the small of my back lowered to cuff the bottom of my ass.

"Donovan—"

"No," he cut me off and answered quickly. "I don't."

"Okay," I whispered softly.

I believed him with everything inside of me, I truly did. I trusted and believed in Donovan.

I just had to ask.

He used to speak of her with pain lacing his tone. Agony would be written all over his handsome, light brown face. During the beginning of our relationship, he was in mourning. Regardless of how badly I piqued his interest the fact remained, she'd hurt him.

"When we met, you were——"

"Distraught more than anything else," he finished. "She crossed me in the worst way. I buried myself in work every day when we were together, so I failed to see that shit coming and I had no one to blame but myself," he explained. "That's what that was, Mona. That's all that was. How can I miss a person who did me like that?"

I rubbed his stomach. "It's possible to miss the good times you shared with a person," I reasoned.

"Yes, it is."

Donovan spread my legs to lie between them. His weight relaxed on top of me warmly, over one-hundred and ninety pounds of an enticing mixture of fat and muscle.

Nothing I couldn't handle.

"But I don't miss them. I'm grateful for how it all went down. That's how I feel at this point. That's the feeling that's taken over the pain. Gratefulness."

"Grateful," I whispered. Darkness surrounded

us, but envisioning his golden-brown eyes staring into mine was easy.

"Grateful it all led me to you."

"Grateful," I repeated once more as his lips debuted on my neck.

Our bare bodies were hot, causing us to pant underneath the linen sheets. The ceiling fan circulating above us provided enough aid to keep us adjoined as our bodies blazed for one another.

"So fucking grateful." He sucked on my bottom lip and rubbed his dick on my clit.

I parted my lips to moan but nothing came out. My mouth was dry until he kissed me, distracting me from his dick at my opening.

"Take it for me," he spoke through a passionate kiss that interrupted my gasp. I spread my legs wider to accept every hard, thick, and painful inch of him. Trapping him against me, I wrapped my legs around his waist.

"I'll always take it for you." I whimpered. Our sex was loud beneath us. My juices orchestrated their own music each time he slow stroked inside of me.

"Yes," I moaned. "Yes. Right there."

Donovan leaned closer to speak into my ear. He

kissed my earlobe before airing a threat that made my nipples harden to the point they ached.

"You should've let me sleep," he said.

I'd not only awakened him; I'd awakened his hunger to fuck me senseless.

I whined when he pulled out of me. I wanted him deeply inside of me again. Deep and steady with his breathtaking strokes.

"Please."

"Every part of your beautiful body deserves my attention," he said.

Donovan tongue-kissed my breasts, circling his tongue around my nipples with his soft, wet lips. After kissing down to my stomach, he glided his lips over my skin.

Between my thighs, he voiced how much he loved me. "Grateful," he uttered from below. His tongue connected with my clit, vibrating up and down at a slow pace that brought tears to my eyes.

My clit pulsated as he feasted, and my legs trembled during every tongue lashing he blessed me with. I fell deeper in love with Donovan every time we made love. Our connection gave sex a new meaning—another way to communicate our unwavering devotion. Just as he loved me like no other, he fucked me like it, too.

Like it would be the last time he enjoyed me, he gave his all whenever he explored my body. He outdid himself like he was in competition with the last time he put it down.

Donovan tapped the side of my thigh twice. Motioning for me to turn over, he massaged my ass cheeks when I did, then spread them to tease my asshole with the tip of his tongue.

I cried through the pleasure. He was the greatest lover I'd ever known. The only man who knew how to exceptionally please every part of me.

Grabbing a fistful of my hair, he held my head back, then grabbed my neck with his free hand.

"I'm sorry." Donovan leaned forward to kiss my cheek. Unable to question his sudden apology, I screamed for mercy as tears cascaded down my cheeks. The head of Donovan's dick was in my ass, arousing both pain and pressure I wasn't ready to endure.

"It's going to be a long night for you," he reminded me.

———

"YOU'RE LATE," MOLLI ANNOUNCED MY ARRIVAL

when I entered our favorite seafood restaurant, Brendon's Catch 23. "As fuck," she added.

All eyes were on us after that. Sitting across from her at our usual table, I smiled at everyone staring our way who looked mortified over her outburst.

"Can you behave? Before I have to beat someone up for judging you and your loud mouth."

"That's what I'm talking about!" She clapped and bounced in her seat. "Ride or die. That's my favorite type of energy."

"Where is Monika? I can't handle you alone today."

I avoided the menu and stashed it aside. I knew exactly what I wanted. Depending on the server taking care of our table, they knew, too. Half of them knew us well. The shrimp platter was one of our favorites. My sisters and I were weekly regulars at Brandon's Catch 23.

"The bathroom. You know she's always pissing like she drinks Malt liquor all day."

"Molli!" I cackled.

Middle child syndrome, I reminded myself. Combine that with her zodiac sign, Virgo, and you were in for a real treat with Molli Samantha Hill.

"Please," I said. "She just drinks a lot of water."

"Fine."

Molli cringed as I cracked my neck. She hated the sound of it. I stretched my arms in front of me and yawned.

"Long night?" she asked.

"You don't want to know. Trust me." I blushed.

"Nasty heffa."

I turned to my left just in time to notice Monika strolling back to our table. Her smile lit up the room. Her chocolate skin glowed amid her pearly white teeth shining and on full display.

"Hey boo." She hugged my neck and kissed my cheek. "Nice of you to join us. I ordered for you already, by the way."

Taking a seat next to me, she fidgeted with her charm bracelet. Molli and I watched her attentively while looking back and forth from each other. Kicking Molli's leg underneath the table, I nodded in Monika's direction.

"What did I miss?" I mouthed silently.

Molli shrugged at me, then placed her focus back on Monika. "Um, Mo. You good?" she asked.

"I'm pregnant," she blurted.

"What?" I screamed, then covered my mouth when heads snapped in our direction again.

"No fucking way," Molli whispered across the

table. Her eyes watered and brought on the water-works from me, too.

"I'm pregnant and I've never been this happy in my life. I found out this morning. My cycle was later than usual, so I begged my doctor to fit me in her schedule. It's really real. She confirmed that I'm six weeks pregnant," she explained.

The perky waitress returned to our table with three strawberry lemonades. "Your food will be out shortly, ladies. Can I get you anything else in the meantime?"

We shook our heads and aired a *thank you* in unison.

"So, Joe finally shot the club up and got you pregnant?" Molli said. "I thought y'all didn't want children."

"Oh, God. Molli." I blew a breath.

"He did what he had to do." Monika danced in her seat. We wiped our eyes before any tears had a chance to fall. Though they were happy tears, we still couldn't go out like that in front of strangers who had their eyes set on our table.

"Congratulations, sis." I wrapped her in my arms. "I can't wait to be an aunt. The favorite aunt."

Molli scoffed before rounding the table to

embrace us in a group hug. "In your dreams, girl," she said to me. "Hopefully, Monika has twins, so we won't have to fight over one niece or nephew."

"Get off me." Monika pushed her away from her. "You went too far."

Molli had always been hardheaded. She hardly listened to anyone other than her unruly thoughts. She rambled on about Monika having twins until our food arrived.

Her light brown eyes gleamed at the shrimp platter and King crab legs the waitress placed before her. She'd gotten those beautiful eyes from our father, along with her flawless, butterscotch skin.

"All I'm missing now is Blove's sauce. I love her YouTube channel!" She licked her lips as she searched through her large purse.

We already knew what time it was.

"Please, Mol. No," I said. "Not here. Not today.

"This lunch is supposed to be special," Monika included.

"It *is* special," Molli exclaimed at the same time she retrieved her phone. Her obsession with Mukbangs was sick, tiring and…

"Unbelievable." Monika sighed. "She's about to

go live and act like she's recording a Mukbang again."

"Hey, Facebook." Molli smiled at the front camera, checking herself out in the process.

"Who still goes live on that nursing home app anyway?" Monika sneered.

"It's the same bitches." Molli shrugged. "The same bitches on every site," she clarified.

"Don't get her started," I whispered to Monika.

"*Why we gotta be bitches,*" Molli read a comment from her live stream. "My bad," she responded to the comment and laughed.

"I damn sure wouldn't be her friend on there. That's why I deleted her ass," Mo whispered to me. "She kept tagging me in everything."

"She still tags you in everything. Friend or not," I advised her.

"I'm with my sisters at Catch 23 on fourth—"

Molli stopped talking and ended her stream without another word, then placed her phone face down on the table. Monika and I stopped whispering to each other to look up at her.

"Mol, you okay?" I asked.

"Hold that thought. I'll be right back." Monika stood up and rushed from the table. Molli's eyes were stuck on her back until she disappeared down the long hallway that led to the restrooms.

"He was on my live," she said.

"Who?"

"Grayson… was on my live."

"What did he say?" I asked after picking my mouth up from the table.

"He said, and I quote, *after searching Facebook for Molli Hill all day, I finally found the right one, the most beautiful one on here.*"

"That was cute. I'm a little impressed," I admitted.

"I'm turned on." She stared at the back of her phone in awe.

"Then why'd you end your live Mukbang like that?"

Molli flashed her middle finger at me. She made sure to change the subject before Monika returned and plopped down beside me again.

"Promise us something, Mo," Molli said. "Don't tell Mom and Dad the good news until we're all there. Mona and I don't want to miss out on anything."

"Yes," I chimed in. "I agree. Especially since Mom ends every call with…"

"*When are you going to give me and your father a grand-child?,*" we all recited her favorite question in unison.

"Yeah." Monika laughed. "We all deserve to be there for this. I wouldn't have it any other way," she promised. "Enough about me." She wiped her glossy eyes. "Molli, how is the new book coming along? You're always working on something."

Molli dipped her crab meat in a small bowl of butter and smiled. Talk of her craft always brought a genuine smile out of her.

"I'm currently in the process of outlining a new project. I start a new book soon. Pray for me," she said.

"We always do. Trust me," I quipped.

"And you?" Monika popped a small shrimp in her mouth and looked my way. "Is your work environment getting any better? Are you and Donovan okay?"

"Work is… work." I scoffed and swallowed hard. "It's never really the job," I explained. "It's always the shitty ass people who work there."

"That's why you need to start your own busi-ness," Molli said. "We're ready to help in any way we can."

"I know that's right," Monika agreed.

Monika ran her graphic design business from

home, with the help of her husband. I sometimes envied my sisters for doing their own thing. They were strong-willed and a bit braver than me. They were motivated creators.

Sadly, I couldn't relate.

Despite loathing the people at my job, I was comfortable. Too comfortable to step out on faith and start my own business.

"I promise to work on it soon," I said.

Anything to get them off my back.

"Great." Monika shook me, excited. "And you and Donovan are fine? I know someone who can take care of that little *problem* for you."

"Mo." I gasped and stared at her with wide eyes. She was serious. Too serious. I shouldn't have laughed, but I couldn't help myself.

"We're great. His ex is out of the picture and I don't think she'll pop up again."

"She'd better not," Molli said, giving Monika a knowing look.

For her sake, I hoped she didn't pop up again.

Chapter 12

I bowed my head and prayed over my lunch. Airing a deep sigh, I opened my eyes to Grayson standing in the threshold of my office, staring at me with a devious smile on his face.

"So much for eating in peace," I mumbled.

Approaching my desk, he kicked the door closed behind him.

"I need your help," he said. I stabbed my knife through my medium-rare steak and leaned back in my chair. "Damn, can I elaborate first?"

Grayson never asked for help pertaining to work. He hardly asked for favors or assistance when he needed it most. I had a feeling I knew what I was in for.

I need you and Mona to double date with me

and Molli," he blurted. He'd spoken too fast for me to keep up with, but it all came together for me in the end.

"You really don't think straight when it comes to her, huh? That woman has you losing your damn mind."

"Don't do too much." He kissed his teeth.

"Am I missing something? Did you cop her number?"

Grayson plopped down in a seat before my desk and huffed. "Look, man. I searched for her on Facebook. Took me a whole day to find her pretty ass. I sent her my number. She accepted the bait."

"You searched her on Facebook?" I chuckled in my fist. "You don't even like to get on that shit to promote the Smokehouse." Grayson despised social media, and he never worked hard to catch a woman's attention. This was new.

"If you don't want to help me just say that." He was in his feelings, too. Another shocker.

Who is this man?

"You're obviously feeling her, G. Why would you want to double date instead of being alone with her? No competition, no interruptions, and no outside company."

"You think I want to share my time with her?

She's fucking beautiful, man. I want her all to myself. Her attention, her brown eyes, all that!"

Grayson jumped up and paced back and forth in front of the door. I couldn't pretend I wasn't entertained. This was an interesting episode in his life. I picked my fork up to take a bite of my steak. The episode was getting good.

"She's hesitant of me. She thinks I'm a player. Her sister got her thinking that I'm a fucking gigolo."

I coughed, then patted my chest to gather myself. "Aye. Mona just nosy. My bad about—"

"I don't care about none of that." He waved me off. "I'm just…" Grayson stopped pacing and stood in place. He combed his fingers through his beard in deep thought. "I've never wanted a woman the way I want her. I'm willing to show her there's more to me than *fucking and ducking*."

"That's what she calls it?"

"Yeah, man." He smiled to himself. "You should've heard her pretty ass trying to tell me about myself over the phone. She thinks she has me all figured out. She has no idea."

"Double dating isn't it," I said, bringing him back to reality. Grayson was getting lost in his thoughts of her. Molli had him on one, for real.

"How about you shut the restaurant down early one night. Have a chef of your preference make you look good. Take that extra step for her. Let her see what she does to you, instead of trying to explain her affect on you. We know women don't listen, so don't waste your time pleading your case. Show her."

Grayson nodded while rubbing over his beard. "I knew I kept you around for something. I fuck with that idea. Let me see if Des is up for making some extra bread."

"Yeah. Go check that out so I can eat in peace," I said.

————

"Welcome home, handsome," Mona cooed. I'd worried she wouldn't be in place after I advised her of a late night at the Smokehouse, but she was exactly where she needed to be. In my space that was slowly becoming our space.

"What's up, beautiful?" I ditched my bag on the floor by the door to get to her. "Damn." I bit my fist at the sight of her. Her dark brown skin was bare, and her hair was tied up and out of her face—away from her neck, just the way I liked it. I didn't mind when her hair was down, but when it was up, her enticing neck was exposed. My access to it was uninterrupted.

Against the red, six-inch heels she wore, the glitter nail polish on her toes sparkled.

"What are you trying to do to me, woman?"

She had a bad ass walk in heels. Almost like she channeled a supermodel on a runway. That shit hypnotized me within seconds.

Approaching me slowly, Mona extended her hand for mine. Her legs glistened, and my mouth watered to savor every inch of her body.

"I'm returning the favor," she said, leading me to the bedroom. "Come. I've started your shower. The temperature is just how you like it.

"Will you be joining me?" I slapped her bouncing ass.

"Yes. If you'll have me." She spun around on her heels to secure her arms around my neck.

"I don't want anyone else."

Our intense eye contact spooked me each time. It was like Mona saw right through me. She understood me and my heart. Mona felt my love for her. I wondered if that shit was as overwhelming for her as it was for me.

"Mona." I stared at her lips, trying to find the right words to express my appreciation.

"I love you too, Donovan. I'll love you forever."

I couldn't wait to get her in the shower with me. Picking her up, I threw her over my shoulder. She squealed when I snatched her heels off, tossed them aside, and then pulled the shower curtain back.

Reuniting at the end of the day felt virtuous. She fit into my life, my heart and my world perfectly.

"Let me get your back out the way, so I can stare at you." She kissed my chest, then motioned for me to turn around. "Do you believe in forever, Donovan?" she whispered from behind me.

"Yeah," I said, turning around to face her. "I believe in it now more than ever."

Mona stroked my dick with a satisfied smile on her beautiful face. "We'll get there," she said. "Forever."

Chapter 13

MONA

Donovan was a beautiful man, especially when he was asleep. During his slumber, his handsome face was relaxed and his brown skin was flawless like silk. I traced his eyebrows with my thumb, smiling at his light snores. I loved waking up before him to enjoy him like that.

He always sensed when I was awake after a while, but I cherished the times he was motionless and relaxing in my arms.

He was safe with me and I was safe with him. Together, we were secure in each other's embrace.

"Donovan," I whispered the moment he stirred in his sleep.

"Hm?"

"Good morning," I chimed, caressing his cheek.

"Good morning, beautiful. What time is it?"

"An hour before we have to get up and deal with people." Donovan groaned and pulled me closer to his warm body. "Can we talk?" I asked.

His eyes shot opened as he studied my expression. "What do you have for me?" He pushed my messy hair out of my face.

"Do you know where Grayson is taking Molli for their date tonight?"

"You can't be serious right now. You just can't be."

"Oh, but I am." I climbed on top of him. "I was going to ask you last night but—"

"Is that what that was? A bribe for information? That's foul."

"That wasn't all it was." I tried to caress his cheek again, but he caught my hand and squeezed it in his. "Don't be like that."

Placing the back of my hand to his lips, he kissed up my arm, distracting me until he flipped me onto my back.

"Mind your business, Mona. Grayson will take care of your sister."

"Fine." I pouted. "It's not like she asked me to find out or anything."

Molli had filled me in on her and Grayson's

progress. She asked me to play Inspector Gadget before their first date. Grayson told her it was a surprise and we hated those. We were way too nosy for surprises. I had to at least try to help her out.

"She'll pay for that. I'm telling G she got you doing her dirty work."

"Suit yourself." I smashed my lips into his. "Snitch."

Donovan pinned me to his king-sized bed by my wrists. His large palms trapped my wrists as he placed soft kisses along my neck.

"Take it back."

"Nope." I moaned, squirming underneath him. My pussy was wet and always prepared for him, but I was caught me off guard when he entered me. I gasped as he parted my lips with his tongue for a passionate kiss.

"I take it back," I said, pleading for mercy.

Gazing into my eyes, he stroked slowly inside of me, pushing deeper and deeper with each stroke. He glanced down to smirk at my lips before staring into my eyes again.

"Focus on us," he said. "I will never let anyone hurt you. That includes the people close to you. I know it'll affect you, and that will fuck with me, too. I'll always protect you and yours. You understand?"

Without waiting for a response, he flipped me onto my stomach.

Donovan handled me well, controlling me during the best times. Knowing all of my spots, he ruled my body, specializing in thoroughly pleasing me. Flat on my stomach, I screamed in pleasure into a pillow, accepting everything he had to offer.

"I love you," he pulled my head back by my hair to utter the spine-chilling sentiment in my ear.

It pained me that those were the three words we had to settle for. Coming from him, the sentiment meant the world to me, but if there were something deeper I could've responded with, I would've recited it in a heartbeat.

My actions would have to fill that missing void.

My touch would have to reassure him of my unwavering love and devotion.

———

A LONG DAY AT THE OFFICE TURNED INTO AN EVEN longer night at the office. Paperwork surrounded my desk and overwhelmed me.

Slapping my pen down, I massaged my temples and sighed. If I could rewind time, Donovan would be lying between my thighs telling me how much he loved me. Since I wasn't that lucky at the moment, my recollections would have to suffice until I encountered him again.

Going against my rule to focus on work, I reached into my top drawer for my phone. Four missed calls from Molli caught my attention before anything else. I studied the time on the right corner of my laptop, noticing she was half an hour into her date with Grayson. It had certainly surpassed the time she told me their time together would commence.

What is going on?

That was the question I asked the moment she answered the phone. Molli panted over the phone like she was undergoing a mid-life crisis.

"Hello? Molli. What the hell?"

"I'm failing at this, Mona. The man is charming. A total sweetheart. Such a gentleman and I'm failing. Shit. I'm more awkward than usual."

"I didn't even know that was possible."

"Me either," she whispered harshly. "Help me. Save me. Come get me. Do something!"

"You don't want that," I said. "You really like him. I can tell, so you just need to be yourself. Take a deep breath. Stop trying to impress him, and be yourself, Mol."

"How do I stop trying to impress a man that fine? I know I'm the ultimate catch but got damn!"

"He is not all that."

"He's at the door," she panicked. "What do I do?"

"Where are you?"

"At the Smokehouse. We have the restaurant to ourselves. Well, besides the chef who's catering to us, we're alone. But I'm hiding in the bathroom right now."

"My goodness! Goodbye, Molli. Leave out of the bathroom. Have a good time and be yourself!" I disconnected our call before she could respond. She was making it really hard for me to mind my business. As things between her and Grayson progressed, I wanted to pry in their business.

It was too bad I couldn't talk and gossip to Monika about it. Molli and I preferred to wait it out when it pertained to discussing a potential lover with her. Out of the three of us, she was the most overprotective sister. Overbearing, too. And sometimes judgmental.

My phone vibrated and *'**Bitch!**'* was the text displayed on my screen. Molli despised being hung up on, but it was for her own good. I was confident she would thank me later.

Bypassing all other notifications, I selected my text thread with Donovan. We were both stuck in our offices, catching up on work that we'd put off for each other. Loving on one another was priority. No, it didn't pay the bills, but if it could, Lord knows I would never see the light of day. His black-out curtains would shield us from the real world every day, all day.

A text from him came through as I re-read our adoration for each other.

Donovan: Let me hear your voice.
Nope.

I should've known better than to deny him. My office phone rang less than a minute later.

"Donovan," I answered, laughing at his nerve. "I said no."

"I can't get fired, and you're one of the best things that's ever happened to that company, so let's say fuck this shit now. Come to me."

"You're so bad." I shook my head and blushed.

"I can't do that. *We* can't do that."

"Then open the door."

"What?" I stood up quickly from my chair. "You're here? How?"

Donovan invited himself inside of my office. After locking the door behind him, he dropped his phone from his ear and stuffed it into the pocket of his slacks. "I slipped security a fifty-dollar bill. Money talks."

"With his cheap ass. That's how much my safety means to him? Fifty-dollars? If he ever hassles me about forgetting my badge again, I'll tell on him."

"Who's the snitch now?" he asked, reeling me into his arms.

"Hey." I punched his shoulder. "Take that back."

"Kiss me first," he said. It took me no time at all to oblige. I rose on my toes to reach his full lips, then tugged on the collar of his shirt for him to meet me halfway.

"What are you doing here?" I paused our tongue war to breathe. "We both said we had a lot of work to catch up on today."

"I can't help that I'm fucked up about you." He sat behind my desk, patting his lap for me to take a seat. "I couldn't focus on work. I can't shake you." Donovan lowered the side handles of my chair and cuffed my ass after I straddled his lap. "Tell me you don't miss me, and I'll go back to work right now."

"We don't lie to each other," I said, resting my head on his shoulder.

"Right."

Even the smile in his tone was contagious.

"I've been thinking about starting my own business," I blurted in a whisper.

"Let's act on it."

"You don't know the details yet." I looked up into his eyes.

"The details will come, I'm sure." He cupped both sides of my face. "I believe in you. I know what you can do. Let's act on it."

"Thank you." He probably had no idea what I was thanking him for. It wasn't only for believing in me, it was for everything he was—everything he brought to the table. "For everything," I finished.

"Thank you." He kissed my forehead and held onto me tighter. In his arms, I belonged.

"You know, you could always take over the financial reports for the Smokehouse. That is, until you start your business. We could use your expertise."

Our fingers were intertwined and linked like our loyalty and devotion to each other.

"The pay can be whatever you feel you deserve. You also get good dick at your request and a pay bonus every week."

"Damn." I stared at him, impressed. "It's killing me to turn that offer down."

"Then don't. Accept the offer."

"I wouldn't get any real work done. Unlimited dick at my request? I already know how good it is. I'll want it all the time. Trust me, this is a bad idea."

"In other words, you're telling me you wouldn't be able to control yourself."

"That's exactly what I'm telling you."

His smile captivated, soothed, teased and made my day all at once.

"I understand." His large hands roamed underneath my skirt. "What did I tell you about wearing these out of the house?" His complaint about my thong aired deep in my ear.

"I was in a rush and grabbed the first thing I saw." Donovan ripped the thin strap from around my waist.

"No need to be jealous," I said. "I've never wanted to belong to anyone until I met you. I'm yours. Believe me."

"Trust me, I believe you."

Chapter 14

"Home sweet home." Mona laid next to me in bed and wrapped her arms around me.

She purred as I massaged her scalp. "I had to drag you out of there before you got the shakes."

"I dream of having your children, Donovan," she said, gathering my full attention. "I've never met a man who fit the card like you. One who compliments my daydreams perfectly. We've moved at a rapid pace, but it feels like we've known each other forever. It really does." She took a deep breath, then exhaled deeply.

"One day, I want us to find a home we fall in love with and make it ours," she continued. "I'm all over the place right now, I know. But the point is, I want everything with you. Everything."

Her voice faded, then she snored lightly. She'd fallen asleep that quickly on my chest.

"I want everything with you too, Mona," I said, willing to repeat it when she woke up. Mona kept my heart full, my pride intact, and my emotions craving her every minute of every day.

A hard-working woman who went out of her way to make sure her family and loved ones were happy, deserved the world. I was equipped to give it to her.

I slipped from under her carefully without interrupting her slumber. In the kitchen, I leaned against the marble countertops and pondered everything Mona said.

Beautiful babies and a home together were music to my ears. We wanted the same things, but I needed more than that.

She'd forgotten one major thing.

Eventually, Mona needed to become my wife. She could take all the time she needed, but I was set on that outcome.

"You left me." Mona stalked into the kitchen and walked directly into my arms.

I chuckled to myself. Sleeping without each

other was hard for us. Once we sensed emptiness beside us, it was a wrap. We sought out for each other immediately.

"Why are you up, beautiful? You're tired. It's all over you." I kissed her forehead.

"In other words, I look a hot ass mess?"

"That's crazy talk. You always look beautiful."

Silence fell between us as I rested my head on top of hers and closed my eyes. I hadn't believed in perfection until I encountered her.

This.

Us.

Everything she stood for.

Perfection.

"Tell me something. Do your dreams include us being married?" I asked. She looked up quickly to search my eyes. "Because mine does. So, clarification," I mentioned. "I need that."

"Yes," she whispered. "That's a part of the everything I want with you."

Kissing her was better than any response I could've mustered. Our fervency spoke for itself.

"Let me get you back to bed." I smiled and rubbed my bottom lip that she'd aggressively bit.

"Don't leave me this time." She looped her arm in mine.

"Never again."

Mona released my arm to walk ahead of me. She lifted my oversized T-shirt above her head and threw it across the room.

"Come put me to sleep." She laid across the bed and spread her legs.

"Sleep?" I rubbed my hands together. "I don't know about that anymore."

At this rate, she would never get the rest she needed.

———

"How did it go, man?" I passed the ball to Grayson and he caught it at the last minute. G was hardly paying attention to our game or keeping score of his own shots. We were only fifteen minutes in and he'd already checked out.

"G." I waved my hand in his face. "Earth to G. How did it go?" I asked for the fifth time.

"Magic, Don. It was dope." He grabbed my shoulders and shook me. His excitement spooked me a bit. He was happier than I'd ever saw him.

"Get this." He covered his smile with the side of his fist. "She ended up staying the night with me. It just happened like that."

"We didn't have sex. I didn't even attempt to, man. I want all of her when the time is right. The time isn't right yet."

I stole the ball from him. "Are you feeling okay?"

"Leave me alone, D." He laughed.

"I'm glad it went well, brother." I dapped his fist. "You deserve that."

"I appreciate you." He pulled me into a brotherly hug and patted my back. "Them damn Hill sisters, huh?" He stole the ball back from me and jogged down the court to dunk it.

"Yup," I muttered behind him. "Welcome to my world!"

Epilogue

MONA

Seven weeks later...

"Why am I so nervous?" Molli pointed to herself. "I'm not the one telling them I'm pregnant."

"Shh! Keep your voice down," Monika whispered.

We were standing outside of our parent's house, mentally preparing ourselves for Monika's special announcement. We'd made her promise to include us in it. Molli and I wanted to witness their excitement. Janice and Morris Hill had been impatiently waiting on their first grandchild for years now.

Their time had finally come.

"You just be sure you're being careful with

Grayson. wouldn't want you to have an announcement next. Out of wedlock, at that."

Me and Molli stared at each other and rolled
our eyes behind her back. That was exactly why we
stalled on telling Monika about the things going on
in our love lives. Our big sister was cool when she
wanted to be. However, she was judgmental when
we least expected it.

"She's lucky she's pregnant," Molli whispered to
me after Monika left us at the bottom step. "I
almost pushed her bloated ass in the grass," she
said. "And you know it's filled with Theo's shit," she
muttered, referring to our mother's poodle.

"Be nice."

"I can't do this." Monika backed away from the
door and returned to the bottom step. "Do you
think they'll suspect something before I get the
chance to tell them?"

"Duh." I laughed. "We're all here. Together.
That doesn't just happen these days."

"Why are we even trippin'? Mom and Dad are
going to flip out in the best way possible," Molli
said.

"That's exactly what we're trying to prepare
for." Monika nodded.

"Is Joe coming to share the amazing news with you?" I asked.

"Unfortunately, he couldn't find anyone to fill in for him at work. If he can't find anyone to watch his security post, he has to be there no matter what." Tears brimmed in her big brown eyes.

Molli moved closer to her and pulled Monika to her side for a hug. "It's okay. We're here with you. You know Joe does what he has to do for his family." She smiled and rubbed Monika's stomach.

"That he does," Monika agreed, placing her hand over Molli's. "I never told y'all this, but Joe and I have been trying to conceive for a while. All this time, I thought something was wrong with me." Tears cascaded down her cheeks, but she swiped them away quickly. "Hell, I wondered if something was wrong with him. I prayed to God that Joe's soldiers were marching strong and healthy, if you know what I mean."

"Jesus, Mo," Molli whispered. "Spare us those type of details."

"Anyway." Monika playfully pushed Molli. "It's finally happening. I'm pregnant. I'm having a baby. It's really happening. *Finally*. I've reached my second trimester and it's time to tell Mom and Dad."

We pulled each other into a group hug. The world stopped as we held on to one another. We closed our eyes and stood still as the limp branches on the scenic trees above our parent's home swayed in the wind.

"It's like Mom and Dad always told us…" I said.

"*God's timing is impeccable*," we finished in unison.

"Yes, yes, it is." Monika wiped her glossy eyes and smiled. "All right. Let's do this."

This time when she approached the door, she actually knocked on it. Molli and I stood behind her, anticipating our father to answer the door. He was our mother's protector. Mom was always behind him watching their backs as he guarded their front. I admired their will to take care of each other.

Looking better, stronger, and younger than the last time we visited, Dad opened the door and smiled at the sight of Monika. "Hey there, sweetheart," his southern accent boomed.

Regardless of how long he'd resided in Louisville, our father was from the south—from a small, country town in Lake Helen, Florida. His accent wasn't going anywhere, and I was grateful for it. His stern accent had gotten me together many times. I couldn't envision a conversation with him without it. It was stuck in my head and deeply rooted in my childhood memories.

"Why didn't you just use your key and come on in?" He pulled her closer for a hug, then his eyes widened when he noticed me and Molli standing behind her. "All my girls are here," he boasted. "Just in time."

He really didn't have to tell us that we were on time for dinner. We knew. The three of us were greedy, and we always based our plans around consuming a delicious meal. Besides, we could smell my mother's infamous fried chicken from outside the door.

"Move along so I can hug my daddy, girl." Molli's rude ass pushed Monika aside to steal the show. She was not only a daddy's girl, but a mommy's girl, too. In other words, she was a kiss ass. A suck up! A favorite of theirs. I was their baby girl and still found myself hating on their bond with Molli sometimes.

"Hey, Dad." I kissed his cheek and glided by them to find Mom. She was already smiling when I entered the kitchen; her arms were wide open for me.

"How are you, baby girl?" She rubbed my back and squeezed me tightly in her arms.

"I'm great, Mom. How are you? Did you shake that cold?"

"Knocked that cold right out of here with some tea and honey. Oh, and my chicken noodle soup. That cold didn't stand a chance." Her warm smile made me feel good every time I saw it.

My mother's presence contained healing powers on its own. Whether I was physically sick or mentally down, she turned a negative into a positive by doing the bare minimum. By simply smiling. To me and our family, she was that powerful.

"You have it smelling good in here." I licked my lips as she turned away from me to pull cornbread muffins out of the oven. They smelled amazing. I was certain they had a perfect mixture of sweetness in them.

"You and your sisters don't show up often together, but when you do, you make sure you're on time," she quipped and looked back to side-eye me.

"Mom, don't do that. We don't only show up for your cooking. We come to check on you and Dad, too. Because we miss y'all and need to frequently reunite as a family."

"Girl, get a stick of butter from the fridge and

roll it over these muffins. Who do you think you're foolin'?

I did as she said without another word. Molli and Monika entered the kitchen laughing loudly with Dad. Molli kissed Mom's cheek, then stood beside me and watched me butter the cornbread muffins with dancing eyes. They were her favorite.

"Mom." Monika gasped. At once, everyone snapped their necks in the direction of the gasp. Mom's hand rested on Monika's stomach. "How did you—"

She was pulled into a hug before she could finish her question. Our mother screamed and rocked Monika from side to side as she cried tears of joy.

"Oh, Morris. Our baby is pregnant. I prayed for this," she said. It was all she exclaimed over and over again.

I prayed for this.

"Does that conclude the announcement?" Molli mumbled to me. I nudged her arm, then looped mine in hers as we, including Dad, gathered around Mom and Monika for a family hug. Though I saw her announcement going another way, the moment remained priceless.

Soon, there would be a new addition to our small, loving family. The feeling was indescribable.

————

I TRAVELED TO THE SMOKEHOUSE TO FIND HIM.

He told me he would be working late, and that he would make it back to me much later in the night. But I couldn't wait.

Could I ever?

I never really could with Donovan. I wasn't that much of a patient woman. Not when it boiled down to waiting around to see him.

No way!

The night was quiet and still with a perfect breeze that blew my hair all over my face until I reached the glass door of the restaurant. When I stopped in front of it, the wind settled down. The serenity of the calm night brought me peace.

After having an amazing dinner with my family, I needed to share my joy with the love of my life.

Everything came back to him. I was certain he was the one for me, positive Donovan was the man I was destined for.

I tapped on the glass door and within seconds,

his tall, toned body appeared in front of the glass door. His eyes lit up as they gazed into mine.

Donovan's bushy eyebrows furrowed as he looked me over. Unlocking the double doors, he pushed one opened and motioned me inside with a nod.

"Are you okay?" he asked, locking the doors behind me. He peered outside, checking the surroundings for a trace of trouble.

"I'm fine." I threw over my shoulder as I made a beeline to his office.

"Mona," he called behind me. It didn't take his long strides any time to catch up with me. He stood in the threshold of his office and stared at me.

I sat on his desk and spread my legs, providing space for him to stand between them.

"What is it?" He stood between my legs and gripped my chin. Donovan held my head in place to face him. "What happened?"

"You happened." I held him close. "And I had an amazing day."

"Then why are you crying?"

"I'm happy. Really happy. And you're a big part of that. You add onto it. You…"

I fell speechless.

Expressing myself to him got harder every day.

The more I fell in love with him, the more difficult it became to express my love to him.

"You," he said. "You, Mona," he whispered in my ear. "I got something for you."

Pulling a black, suede box from his pocket, he opened the top and exposed a rose gold, diamond ring. A cluster of small, white, round diamonds decorated the center, and additional small diamonds flowed along the rose-gold band.

The beauty of it stumped me.

Was I shallow for contemplating how many carats the ring was?

I couldn't help myself. Just like I couldn't help that more tears fell from my eyes.

"Listen to me, beautiful. And understand me while you're at it, okay?"

I nodded.

"This isn't a proposal. Trust me, I would shut the city down for that shit. I would get on both knees and beg the Lord to stop time until you said yes. You deserve all that. This..." He retrieved the ring from its slot and ditched the box. After reaching for my right hand, he eased the spectacular diamond ring on my ring finger.

"This is a promise. A promise that we're just getting started and have a lifetime to go. A promise that you and I will continue to build and reach every milestone we've ever dreamed of… together. A promise that I'll love you more every day. A promise that with me, you're safe. Physically, mentally, and emotionally. You're safe with me, Mona."

"Donovan." I exhaled deeply and covered my mouth.

"A promise to love you when it hurts." He kissed my cheeks again, kissing away more tears. "We'll be here until morning if I recite all my promises, but it's all good. I wrote them down for you."

Reaching behind me, he grabbed a yellow notepad from his desk. Pages of promises took up three, full pages. My heart fluttered.

"The ultimate promise ring." He admired the glistening ring on my finger before planting a kiss on top of my hand. "I can't wait to marry you, Mona. Ever since you mentioned having my children, it's all I can think about. I know it'll all come together for us, because I don't plan on letting you go. Until it's time to experience everything we want with each other, let's start your financial business. Let's spend another year loving each other like we've never loved before. Let's build."

"Yes," I whispered with a wide smile that

burned my cheeks. "Let's." I moaned when his lips connected with my neck. "You're so good to me." I closed my eyes and basked in the allure he projected onto me.

"A promise to be even better to you," he whispered in my ear, driving me crazier than I already was about him. "I never want to stop adding onto your happiness."

"I love you, Donovan Powell."

"I promise to love you forever, Mona Hill."

The end

Now, tell me, would you like to hear more from Molli and Grayson?

Author's Note

Thank you for reaching the end of Mona x Donovan's story! I am excited to discuss their journey with you. If you've enjoyed this book, please consider leaving a review on Amazon + Goodreads

Here are some goodies to enjoy:

Guarded by Love's Apple Music Playlist: https://music.apple.com/us/playlist/guarded-by-love/pl.u-yZyVW5lFDW4B0D

Guarded by Love's visual Pinterest Board: https://pin.it/kuzpv2tzg3gftf

Join us in my readers group on Facebook to share your thoughts on Guarded by Love: http://bit.ly/ShaniceRomanticHaven

You can also connect with me on my personal Facebook here: http://bit.ly/FBShaniceSwint

To be the first to know of new releases, cover reveals, giveaways and more, subscribe to my mailing list here: http://eepurl.com/dsb1EL

Again, thank you so much for indulging in Mona x Donovan's story. I can't wait to hear from you.

xoxo, ShanicexLola

CPSIA information can be obtained
at www.ICGtesting.com
Printed in the USA
LVHW051946171220
674450LV00014B/1513

9 798655 626140